# The Poetry of Murder

# The Poetry Of Murder

## Bernadette Steele

Oak Tree Press  Taylorville, IL

THE POETRY OF MURDER, Copyright 2008, by Bernadette Steele, All Rights Reserved. Printed in the United States of America. No part of this book may be used or reproduced in any manner whatsoever without written permission except in the case of brief quotations used in critical articles and reviews. For information, address Oak Tree Press, 140 E. Palmer St., Taylorville, IL 62568.

Oak Tree Press books may be purchased for educational, business or sales promotional purposes. Contact Publisher for quantity discounts

First Edition, January 2008

10 9 8 7 6 5 4 3 2 1

Cover by MickADesign.com

This book is intended for entertainment purposes only, and all the characters and situations are purely the invention of the author. Any similarity to real persons, living or dead, is purely coincidental.

### Meet the Author Opportunities

If you are a book club, organization, educational institution, faith-based group, library or company, and you would like to schedule a speaking engagement with the author, please send an e-mail message to her at: author@bernadettesteele.net

Library of Congress Cataloging-in-Publication Data

Steele, Bernadette, 1970-
 The poetry of murder / by Bernadette Steele.
  p. cm.
 ISBN-13: 978-1-892343-08-6 (alk. paper)
 ISBN-10: 1-892343-08-8 (alk. paper)
 1. Inheritance and succession--Fiction. 2. Women college students--Fiction. 3. Aunts--Crimes against--Fiction. 4. African Americans--Fiction. 5. University of Chicago--Fiction. I. Title.
 PS3619.T433P64 2007
 813'.6--dc22
                    2007040051

# Dedication

To Cathyne for her support
and encouragement

# CHAPTER 1

As Victoria completed the thank you cards, day turned to night and the danger of the snow was approaching fast but so was the beauty that came with its arrival. Victoria gazed out of the window at the Midway Plaisance as the first winter storm of the year hit Chicago. The longer she looked at the snow, the harder it fell and the whiter the Midway became. The wind rattled the windows in the room as her cell phone rang.

"You want what?"

"I want to talk to you tonight. Meet me in your office."

"It's eleven o'clock. Can't this wait until morning?" Victoria asked.

"No, I'll see you in ten minutes."

Before Victoria could respond, the phone disconnected. She turned the phone off, placed it on the table and walked out of the room past the main hallway of International House and toward the empty front desk.

As she stepped into her office, she felt an arm grab her across the abdomen. She twisted and felt a sharp object enter her right shoulder. She turned her head to look at her shoulder and saw a needle come out of her arm. The arm holding her from behind let go. The room became blurry, and she could only make out the outline of her desk. She tried to rub her eyes, but her arms felt heavy and stiff. The room continued to blur until it finally turned completely dark. She tried to walk but her legs collapsed and she fell. She could feel her limbs, but they would not obey her commands. She tried to scream, but she could not move her mouth. The door closed behind her.

Blind and paralyzed, she lay on the floor for what seemed like an eternity on her right side, slightly bent over at the waist. The door opened again. She heard the slow and steady breath of a person in the room with her. She felt two arms slide under her armpits and straighten out her upper body. The person walked to where her feet were and grabbed her ankles and began to straighten her legs. She felt that her body was now lying perfectly straight on her back. Even though the floor in her office had plush, thick carpeting, the floor seemed to get harder by the second.

Two gloved hands took off her right shoe, and then her left shoe, unzipped and removed her pants, unbuttoned her blouse and carefully removed her right arm and then her left arm. The hands slid under her buttocks and pulled down her stockings and underwear. The two hands proceeded to unhook her bra and removed it.

The carpet made her bare skin tingle. As a cool draft blew across her naked body, goose bumps popped out on her skin. Her arms were placed at her sides and her hair adjusted around her head.

A cold, sharp object pierced her chest. The pain in her chest quickly traveled to her head and feet. When the person slowly pulled the object out of her chest, a warm liquid spread all over the top and down the sides of her chest. She realized that she had been stabbed in the chest. She heard a voice whisper. "And now nineteen more. One for each year."

*And I will meet you in hell one day*, Victoria thought. And then the pain stopped, forever.

# CHAPTER 2

While drinking a protein drink, Geneva looked out of her window and saw the ground, the trees, and the buildings covered in a white virgin blanket of snow. The best thing about her room at International House was the view it provided of the Midway Plaisance, an eighty acre linear park that connected Washington Park on the west end to Jackson Park on the east end.

Geneva liked living at I-House because she enjoyed living with people from around the world. She liked knowing she walked the same halls and slept in the same room as the late African-American poet, Langston Hughes, had done decades before her birth.

She also liked to live at I-House because her Aunt Victoria served as its director. Victoria Franklin was the forty-eight-year-old, younger half-sister of Geneva's mother. Victoria and Geneva's mother had different fathers but the same mother. Victoria's soft tan complexion, big brown eyes, and six-foot tall extroverted personality were in stark contrast to Geneva's brown complexion, pudgy physique and introverted self. People were often surprised to learn the two of them were related.

Before she went to bed last night, Geneva finished typing the last poem for her next collection. Every time she finished a poem, she felt as if a weight had been lifted off her shoulders. A sense of calmness filled her. She enjoyed writing poetry, but found that she had to force herself to write everyday. Geneva felt guilty if she not did write everyday. Because of her writing fellowship, she no longer had any excuses for not writing except for her private laziness and personal procrastination. The political maneuverings, avalanche of emails, and the long-winded meetings of the corporate world that she endured for eight years as a web site designer were no longer a part of her life. She liked creating and developing web sites, but the uncooperative people, unrealistic expectations, and corporate schizophrenia that accompanied her position, had turned a fun job into a prison sentence.

After she thumbed through her poems, she heard a knock at her door. She opened the door and found Zain.

"So are you still upset with me?" Zain asked as she stepped in Geneva's room.

"No, but I should be. I wish you hadn't told my aunt about why I didn't want to go to Montego Bay with you to visit your mother's family," Geneva said.

"Good, because you shouldn't be upset with me. Thanks to me you're going to Jamaica."

"I'm thirty-five, and I can't keep getting handouts from my aunt. If I can't afford something on my own, then I shouldn't have it."

"She doesn't view it as a handout. She wants to help you."

Geneva wanted to say more, but knew that it would be a futile task. She looked into Zain's eyes. With her task accomplished, Zain's clear chocolate complexion glowed and a smile traveled from her left ear to her right ear. Geneva cherished their friendship, but sometimes Zain could be very one-track minded. She often ignored Geneva's wishes and did whatever it was that Zain thought was best. Geneva told her explicitly not to mention anything to her aunt about her reasons for not going on the trip, but Zain did.

With her new poems in hand, Geneva and Zain took the elevator downstairs to drop them off at Victoria's office. Because of the early morning hour, Geneva knew her aunt would not be in her office yet. Her plan was to simply slide the poems under her door.

"Was your father's travel request approved to visit his family in Havana this year?" Geneva asked.

"No, it was denied. He's disappointed but not surprised," Zain replied.

"Well, at least your family can get together in Jamaica this summer," Geneva said.

They got off the elevator and walked down the main hallway. Geneva continued past the front desk to her aunt's office. The door to Victoria's office was slightly open. Geneva pushed open the door and saw her aunt on the floor, naked and in a pool of blood. Geneva felt her stomach convulse and before her hand reached her mouth, her protein drink gushed from her mouth. Her stomach convulsed again but nothing came up and instead she just gagged, and started to cry. Zain walked up behind her and saw Victoria on the floor. Zain touched Geneva's arm. "What happened?"

Geneva heard Zain's voice, but did not respond. Being careful to avoid Geneva's regurgitated protein drink, Zain walked over to Victoria's body, and stopped just short of stepping into the blood on the floor. She squatted down and placed her hand on Victoria's neck. Zain stood up and turned back toward Geneva. Tears streamed down Geneva's face. She did not speak.

Zain took Geneva's arm. "Let's go into the hallway," Zain said as she directed Geneva out of the office.

Geneva still held the doorknob in her hand. Her legs became weak, and she felt as if she were going to fall down so she clutched the doorknob tighter. Her heart started to beat faster. Zain gently pried Geneva's hand from the doorknob, walked her out of the office, and sat her down in one of the chairs in the hallway. Geneva continued to stare at Victoria's body. Zain walked back over to Victoria's office door and closed it.

Geneva stared at the door to her aunt's office. Zain walked behind the front desk and picked up the telephone and called the police. Geneva sat staring straight ahead, weeping and unable to move. Her aunt Victoria was dead.

# CHAPTER 3

Until the police were ready to question her, one of the officers asked Geneva to sit in the Coulter Lounge. When she first entered the room, the sounds of voices and people walking back and forth drowned out her own thoughts. Now, the voices and footsteps were gone, and she was alone with her thoughts. She wondered if anyone had heard her aunt cry for help? Why would anyone kill her aunt? Who killed her?

The double doors leading into the lounge opened and a woman walked into the room.

"Hello, are you Geneva Anderson?" the woman asked.

"Yes, I am."

"Ms. Anderson, I'm Detective Yvonne Peterson. And I'll be investigating your aunt's death. I'm sorry for your loss. I'd like to ask you a few questions."

The words "your aunt's death," made her eyes well up with more tears. She adjusted herself on the couch.

"How can I help?" Geneva said as she lifted her glasses and wiped her eyes. "Do you know what happened?"

Detective Peterson, a middle-aged, brown skinned woman with shoulder length gray hair, sat on the couch directly across from Geneva. Detective Peterson had beautiful soft brown eyes. Geneva wondered how many dead bodies those eyes had seen.

Detective Peterson reached into her worn Coach shoulder bag and pulled out a notebook and pen.

"No, but we're trying to find out what happened," Detective Peterson replied. She crossed her legs at her ankles, opened her notebook and began to write. "What time did you find your aunt's body?" Detective Peterson continued.

"I found her a little after seven this morning."

"Why were you visiting her so early?" Detective Peterson asked.

"I was dropping off some of my poems."

"Did you see anyone while you were walking to your aunt's office?" Detective Peterson asked.

"No, I didn't see anyone. It's very quiet around here at that hour. People don't usually get up until ten or eleven in the morning."

"Do you know of any personal or professional problems that your aunt was having?" Detective Peterson asked.

"No, my aunt got along with everyone she knew. She was a very outgoing and social person. Everyone on campus knew her."

"How long have you lived here at International House?" Detective Peterson asked.

"For two years," Geneva said.

"Are you a student at the University of Chicago?"

"No, I have a writing fellowship, and I'm writing a book of poetry," Geneva said.

"Did she get along with the staff members here at International House?" Detective Peterson asked.

"To my knowledge, yes. But she never talked about the people that she worked with or even the people at the University."

It was true. Most people make some comment either positive or negative about the place where they work, but not her aunt. Victoria never talked about I-House. When Geneva first moved here, she used to ask her aunt about different staff members and residents, but Victoria would not provide any answers. Eventually, Geneva stopped asking and simply reasoned that her aunt clearly wanted to keep her professional life and personal life separate.

"I see. Where were you last night between the hours of eleven and one in the morning?" Detective Peterson asked.

"I was in bed. I went to bed at ten-twenty," Geneva said.

"When did you last see your aunt?" Detective Peterson asked.

"I last saw her on Saturday night during the New Year's Day dinner."

"Well, I think this all for now," Detective Peterson said as she stood, reached into her purse and pulled out a business card. "Here's my card. In case you think of any thing else, please don't hesitate to call me."

Geneva took the card as she stood. "Will you please keep me informed?"

"Yes, I will, but if you don't hear from me, please, feel free to call me. I have to interview Ms. Valdez now. Would you mind stepping out of the room?"

"Of course." Geneva walked toward the door. Detective Peterson reached the door ahead of Geneva and opened it. Zain was standing outside the door with a police officer next to her. Detective Peterson motioned to Zain to come into the lounge. "You can come in now, Ms. Valdez." Zain walked past Geneva, and they exchanged the eye contact of familiarity but not words.

Geneva took the elevator to the seventh floor and returned to her room where she turned off the lights. She walked directly to her window and squinted her eyes as the sun reflected off the snow. Geneva closed the curtains, took off her glasses, curled up on her bed and started to cry again.

# CHAPTER 4

After spending the past day and a half interviewing the victim's friends, colleagues and neighbors, it became clear that Victoria Franklin had carved out a delicate and refined public persona. But considering the way she was murdered, Detective Peterson was not surprised when another image started to emerge. Peterson spent Tuesday morning reviewing the victim's home, cellular and office phone records. The records revealed that during the thirty days before her death, she received over one hundred calls from the home, cell, and office phones of Bradley Wilson. Wilson was married to Elizabeth Wilson, the resident manager of I-House and one of Franklin's direct reports.

In addition, Franklin's checking account activity revealed that she had another source of income that was miles above and beyond her I-House director's salary. The bank records showed that the victim made regular monthly cash withdrawals of five thousand dollars and received regular monthly deposits in the amount of one hundred thousand dollars. Unfortunately, Peterson could not identify the source of the deposits because they were from a Swiss bank account.

Peterson knew that she stood a better chance of the murderer turning him or herself in than she did of obtaining permission to access the records of a Swiss bank. Thus, her next stop would be Bradley Wilson's office to see if he could shed some light on why a married man would call a single woman one hundred times.

* * *

The building that was home to the Graduate School of Business, with its sparkling glass exterior, was in stark contrast to the campus' mostly gothic limestone architecture. As the manager of the university's multi-billion dollar endowment fund, Wilson's office was appropriately located on the top floor. When she arrived outside of his office door, his secretary's desk was empty; but his office door was cracked just enough for her to see that he was sitting at his desk. As she entered the room, the door creaked and his eyes darted towards the doorway.

"I'm Detective Yvonne Peterson. I'd like to ask you some questions about the murder of Victoria Franklin." She walked into the room and sat in front of his desk. When the goose bumps started at her legs and quickly traveled to her chest as she shivered slightly, she soon realized that the window was open.

"Yes, of course. But I don't know how I can help."

"Ms. Franklin's phone records show that she received over a hundred calls from you during the last thirty days before her death. Why were you calling her so much?"

"Well, I was calling her regarding a fund raising weekend for the endowment. We wanted to have some of our activities at the I-House. But, we were never really able to nail down the details."

"Is that the only reason why you were calling her?"

"Yes, what other reason could there be?"

"You'll have to tell me, Mr. Wilson. Where were you on Sunday night between eleven and one in the morning?"

"I was visiting my daughter. She's in the hospital."

"Which hospital?"

"She's in the U of C Children's hospital."

"What's her name and can she confirm your visit?"

"Her name is Monica and no she's not able to confirm anything. She has been comatose for the past five years."

"Can anyone else confirm your presence at the hospital?"

"Maybe the night nurse or security guards."

"Why were you visiting her so late at night?"

"I always visit her at night. And I don't really pay attention to the time."

"How well did you know Ms. Franklin?"

"Not very well, I'm afraid. You should probably talk to my wife, Elizabeth. She has worked with her for over ten years."

"When is the fund raising event planned?"

"It's not. We decided to go in another direction."

When Peterson left Wilson's office, her senses told her that he had lied to her either about his alibi or why he was calling Franklin or both. She might be able to disprove his alibi depending upon how the hospital tracked its visitors. However, the reason for his calls to Franklin might be a little more difficult to disprove. Wilson was not the kind of man to call anyone about event planning. He hired people to do those sorts of domestic chores. But even if she could prove that he lied to her about his alibi and the calls, she still needed more evidence to link him to the victim. And maybe that would come in the autopsy report.

# CHAPTER 5

The coldness of death radiated through the closed door of autopsy room seven at the Cook County Medical Examiner's office. Detective Peterson looked through the window on the door as she knocked on it. Inside the room, Dr. Raymond Harris who was five feet tall, bald and stocky motioned to her to come into the room. She nodded no and stepped back from the door just as her breath finished fogging up the window. She did not need or want to go into the room. She saw the body at the crime scene and that was enough for her. She just needed the autopsy report.

A few minutes later in the hallway, Peterson was greeted by a bright smile surrounded by a sea of pale skin. Dr. Harris handed her the autopsy report.

"The victim bled to death as a result of being stabbed twenty times in the chest. The stab wounds were random, but not deep enough to kill her instantly. She died slowly. After the last stab wound, I estimate that it took her between thirty-five and forty-five minutes to die. It's my opinion that a long, smooth, narrow object was used to kill her. And this object was not a regular knife," Dr. Harris said.

"Did you find any defensive wounds or fibers under her fingernails?" Peterson asked.

"No, nothing. She didn't have any bruises on her body. She was a tall, physically fit woman. I think she would have fought her attacker. Her attacker came prepared."

Dr. Harris handed Peterson another file. "The toxicology report proves this. She was injected with a drug cocktail. She had norcuron and hexachorophane in her blood stream. There was also a needle mark in her right shoulder."

"What are norcuron and hexachorophane?"

"Norcuron is a neuromuscular blocking agent that can induce paralysis. If enough of it is used, it can paralyze a person's entire body including their face."

"So the killer wanted her to know what was happening to her and to feel as much pain as possible, but not move or see."

"It would appear that way. It's not easy to obtain norcuron and hexachorophone. They can only be purchased directly from the manufacturer, and they're only sold to medical facilities such as hospitals and veternarians."

"Well, then I guess my first step will be to see if any hospitals or manufacturers have some of their inventory missing."

"After that maybe your next stop could be to see if there's a link between this case and the death of Devon Bannister," Dr. Harris said.

Dr. Harris handed her a copy of another autopsy report. "Devon Bannister was a twenty-year-old African American college student who was found dead in a hotel room. He died from an asthma attack, but he had norcuron in his blood stream too. Since it's rare to have two victims both with the same drug in them, there might be a connection," Harris said.

"Yes, there might be. Thanks for pulling this for me," Peterson said.

"In order for the neuromuscular blocking agent to be effective and not fatal, you have to inject an amount that correlates to the victim's height and weight. It's hard to find a woman who is six feet tall but it's easy to find a guy," Harris said.

Peterson looked at Bannister's autopsy report. It showed that both victims were the same height and weight. She knew that Harris was on to something. Bannister could have been a practice murder. But it would be difficult to prove because it was a cold case. Because the autopsy report could not conclusively determine that the neuromuscular blocking agent contributed directly to Bannister's death, and he was a known asthmatic, the cause of death was ruled to be due to an asthma attack. The case was cleared from the books.

In her car, Peterson accessed the department's database and pulled up the official police report. It showed that his grandmother, Angela Bannister, reported him missing. This would be her next stop.

# CHAPTER 6

Angela Bannister lived on the fourth floor of a newly built apartment building for senior citizens located at Eighty-fourth and Cottage Grove. When Detective Peterson approached Mrs. Bannister's door, the aroma of peach cobbler penetrated her nostrils like a cool breeze awakens the skin on a hot day. The mixture of peaches, sugar, cinnamon and fresh crust reminded her how Sunday dinner at her grandmother's house was a little different than it was at the homes of other families because the Petersons ate dessert first and then dinner.

Detective Peterson rang the doorbell and while she waited, she secretly hoped that Mrs. Bannister would offer her some peach cobbler. The door opened and a slim woman with long white hair and a radiant light brown complexion greeted her. The woman confirmed that she was Angela Bannister. The physical condition of her own mother combined with the fact that Mrs. Bannister was a sixty-one-year-old woman who did not look a day over forty-five, reminded Detective Peterson why she maintained a healthy lifestyle. And thus, after she entered the living room and her hostess fulfilled her wish, Detective Peterson graciously, albeit with second thoughts, declined a serving of cobbler.

The living room contained two navy blue winged back chairs with a round mahogany table sitting between them occupied by an eight by ten high school graduation picture of Devon Bannister, an ottoman, a floor lamp, and a television set. There were no paintings on the walls and no other photographs in the room besides Devon's. But what the room lacked in furniture, it more than made up for in plants. The room contained dozens of lush green plants whose presence was magnified by a bouquet of two-dozen pink carnations, which sat in front of the room's middle window. Detective Peterson sat in the chair that was turned slightly towards the windows.

"Why are you so interested now in the death of my grandson?" Mrs. Bannister asked.

"I'm working on another case. The murder of Victoria Franklin," Detective Peterson replied.

"I heard about the Franklin murder on the news. She was stabbed to death in her office. How's her death connected to my grandson's?"

"I'm afraid that I can't get into the details right now. But I'd like to find out some more about Devon."

"When he was murdered, no one cared. He was just another dead black man. But I cared. He did all of the right things. He did well in school, had a job, worked hard, and helped me out when I needed it. But no one cared. I raised him. His parents died in a car crash when he was a baby. I suppose if you don't find anything to help you, then you won't care anymore either."

"I apologize that Devon's case wasn't handled more thoroughly. But I'll do everything I can to find out what really happened to him."

"Don't take this personally, but I don't want a bunch of apologies. It's true that Devon suffered from asthma. But it's also true that someone let my grandson die in that dirty hotel room. I want to know who that someone is."

Yvonne took out her notebook and pen. "Can you tell me about his job at the hospital?"

"He just worked there part-time as an orderly. It was just a job. He went to school part-time at Roosevelt University. He was an accounting major."

"Did he have any problems at work or in school?"

"No, he just used to complain about how boring his job was."

"Did he have any friends at work or school or outside of those two?"

"No, not really. He wasn't very social, not even in high school. He didn't hang out. I raised him to mind his own business. His time was taken up by school and work."

"Did you ever suspect that he had any other problems like gambling, drugs or depression?"

"No, I never suspected anything like that. He wasn't involved in any of those things and he certainly wasn't depressed."

"Did he have a girlfriend?"

"Well, I don't know. He told me that he was dating one of the residents at the hospital. But when I told her about his death, she said that she didn't even know my grandson much less date him. But I don't know why he would lie to me. So, I always thought that she was lying, but I could never prove anything. I couldn't find anyone who ever saw them together."

"What's the resident's name?"

"Her name is Deepa Sharma. She's Indian. You know from India. I didn't like her. She's one of those pretty girls with a snobby disposition."

"What do you mean?"

"She was very short with me and tried to be condescending. Devon wouldn't have anything in common with someone like her."

"How long did he say they dated?"

"Not long. They only went out on five dates before he died. I have to admit that I thought it was odd for a resident to date an orderly but then again, he was a nice young man and very good looking." Mrs. Bannister glanced at his photograph and smiled.

"Do you have any idea about why he was at the Ramada Inn that day?"

"No, I've asked myself the same question since he died. He had an apartment so there was no need that I can see for him to take a woman there."

"Did he have his asthma under control?"

"Yes, he did. He hadn't had an attack for over five years. He didn't use his inhaler that often either. That's why I think someone caused him to have an attack."

Detective Peterson concluded her interview with Mrs. Bannister but before she left, her resolve was tested again when Mrs. Bannister extended another offer to give Peterson some cobbler. She politely but regretfully declined the offer.

# CHAPTER 7

Detective Peterson parked her car in the hotel's lot. She picked up the printout of Deepa Sharma's picture. Using the laptop and portable printer in her car, Peterson accessed the police department's report database before she arrived at the hotel. Sharma did not have a police record, not even a parking ticket for her red BMW. The only interesting thing about Ms. Sharma was that she lived at International House. Was this a coincidence? Maybe, but if there was one thing that she had learned during her five years as a homicide detective, it was that coincidence did not exist and that all situations were created by human intervention.

Paul Jones, the front desk clerk, followed the poor white man's "Look Cool" recipe. He applied a bottle of mousse to his hair, combed it straight back and wore his collar up. But his chubby body and acne scarred face got in the way of his cool look.

"So you remember the murder of Devon Bannister?" Peterson asked.

"I remember them finding a body in one of the rooms. Was it murder? I heard the guy died from an asthma attack. We've never had a murder here before," Jones replied.

Peterson placed the picture of Deepa on the counter in front of Jones. "Do you remember seeing this woman on or before the day that Bannister's body was found?"

Jones picked up the photograph. "I don't remember seeing her here when the guy's body was found. But I've seen her here over the past few weeks."

"You've seen her here recently? Who was she with?"

"I don't know who she was with. I've seen her drive up in her red BMW. I don't want or need to know who visits who at this place."

Detective Peterson had Jones check the hotel records but Sharma's name did not show up, only Devon's name on the day that he checked in.

# CHAPTER 8

Deepa Sharma's Versace shoes tapped on the floor as she made her way to her desk chair and her leather skirt and jacket made a screeching sound when she sat down. Peterson stood. Her hostess did not offer a seat and Peterson choose not to take one. She decided that it would be better if she towered over Sharma.

"I don't know a Devon Bannister," Deepa said.

"He worked as an orderly at the U of C hospital. He was found dead in August 2004," Peterson said.

"All of the orderlies look a like to me. I don't know one from the other much less their names."

"I've been informed that the two of you were dating."

"That's ridiculous. Why would I date an orderly? I can do better than that, I assure you."

*You mean he could've done better*, Peterson thought. "I see. Have you ever been to the Ramada Inn?"

"No, I haven't. I don't know anyone who would stay there."

*There's one lie.* Peterson thought. She did not pursue the hotel matter because the clerk could not place her there when Bannister was there.

"If you should remember anything else, please give me a call." Peterson handed her a card. Deepa took the card, stood and walked toward the door and opened it.

"I don't think you will be hearing from me anytime soon."

"You never know, I might."

After leaving International House, Peterson decided to head down the street to visit her mother. In addition to her regular Sunday visits, she liked to make surprise visits during the week in order to keep the staff alert to her presence. Even though her mother lived in a rather upscale assisted living facility, Peterson still felt the need to keep an eye on the staff because money does not always buy good service.

# CHAPTER 9

Zain watched her sabre glide through the air, heard the steel strike the wood floor with a single clatter and slide to a stop in front of a pair of black leather boots. She did not remove her mask because if she did it would mean that the person wearing the boots would know from whose hand the sword came. She was amazed that after all of these years, she still tried to avoid Heather Whitmore.

Even though Zain did not remove her mask, she could sense that Heather knew the person behind the mask. A smile grew on her face as she bent over, picked up the sword and threw it toward Zain. Zain removed her mask just as the sword landed at her feet.

"Hey, be careful. We don't throw swords here," Chris yelled.

The sound of Chris' voice reminded Zain that a third person was in the studio with her and Heather.

"It's ok, can you excuse us," Zain asked.

"I don't think that's a good idea."

"I insist."

The reluctance in Chris' voice said she wanted to stay but the words coming out of her mouth said she would leave and her body followed. As she walked toward the studio's exit, Heather walked toward Zain. Heather's boots echoed throughout the studio. As Heather continued toward Zain, the four thousand square foot fencing studio with its three walls of ten foot mirrors became like a padded elevator.

"Well, I see that not much has changed since high school. You're still losing your sword," Heather said.

"What are you doing here?"

Zain asked the question even though she already knew the answer. She had seen Zain prowling around the studio before. She was here to recruit fencers for her underground fencing club, The Mouliner, where fencers compete in unregulated bouts.

Heather makes money from the betters who watch the bouts in the basement underneath a gentlemen's club or via online podcasts. The good fencers can make a lot of money. But that's not why they fight. The fencers compete because they enjoy the ability to fence without being bogged down or impeded with a bunch of rules and cables for electronic scoring.

"I'm here looking for talented fencers. Obviously, I'm not here to see you, but I thought I would at least give you back your sword."

"You're not supposed to be here. The captain said that you were banned from the premises."

"Why are you still trying to fence? You know that you'll never live up to your family's legacy. It must be frustrating. Stuck pretending to be a fencer, no boyfriend, living in that tiny room at International House."

"What's frustrating is listening to your babbling. Now are you going to leave or do I have to call the campus police?"

"You can throw me out all you want, but I'll always be able to find fencers who want real fencing."

Although Zain hated to admit it, she knew that Heather was right. Heather turned and walked out the studio.

# CHAPTER 10

As the sunlight beamed through her window, Geneva acknowledged to herself that she did not miss having a job. She realized a long time ago that the need to work was one of those quiet cruelties inflicted by society upon individuals. Society forced people to make a choice between their need to have food, shelter and clothing and their desire to pursue a dream. Without fail, the dream was always the loser.

She woke up at six, but remained on her back in bed while the mournful sounds of the Rockefeller Chapel's carillon signaled the passing of each hour. When the carillon rang in the nine o'clock hour, Geneva threw back the covers and sat on the side of her bed.

She turned and looked at the clock next to her bed. It was eleven-twenty, and she was still sitting on the side of her bed. She needed to get moving. She had to meet Henry Nicholson at one in the afternoon. Henry Nicholson was her aunt's attorney, and he was going to read her will today. Usually wills are read after the funeral of the deceased. But because Mr. Nicholson was going out of town on Friday and would not be back for the next two weeks, he asked if he could read Victoria's will before her funeral.

Geneva had never attended a will reading and did not know what to expect. But she knew that she hated to be late for anything. She quickly cleaned herself up and got dressed. By noon she stepped out her door.

\* \* \*

Her elevator ride to the ninety-fifth floor of the Sears Tower was not only accompanied by the usual ear popping and the need to swallow, but also by the questioning glances of the various people who got on and off the elevator. It's the glance that most African American people get when they enter a place occupied by mostly white people in suits. But when Geneva entered the offices of the Nicholson law firm, she forgot about those questioning looks and instead enjoyed the knowledge that the traditional décor of mahogany walls, antique early American furniture and large baroque paintings were owned by people who looked just like her. The Nicholson law firm was founded and owned by an African American family, a family in its fourth generation of all male children. All four brothers were the firm's senior partners. The youngest brother, Henry Nicholson, was her aunt's personal attorney.

Mr. Nicholson's secretary escorted Geneva into Mr. Nicholson's office. Henry Nicholson was a tall, brown skinned man with slightly graying hair. And like all of the Nicholson men, he had a shining smile that could light up any dark moment.

"Hello, Ms. Anderson. Thank you for coming. Please accept my condolences," Nicholson said.

"Thank you," Geneva replied.

"Victoria spoke of you often. She was very proud of you."

"She was a wonderful woman, and I'll miss her," Geneva said.

"I understand. We will make this as quick and as easy possible. Your aunt took care of everything. You have nothing to worry about. Your aunt always kept her will up to date. You are her sole heir," Nicholson said.

Geneva did not know what to say. She sat in the chair and just listened.

"I see."

"Because you are the only person named in the will, I will simply tell you what your aunt left you. Your aunt left you the sum of her personal estate that has a cash value of ten million dollars. This money is in two accounts. One is a domestic Money Market account and the other is a Swiss bank account. The bulk of the money, six million dollars is in the Swiss bank account. In addition, your aunt had an insurance policy in the amount of five-hundred thousand dollars, and your half sister is the sole beneficiary on it. Because you are the sole heir to her personal estate, she did not feel that it was necessary to include you on the insurance," Nicholson said.

Geneva adjusted herself in her chair. Did she hear him correctly, ten million dollars and a half sister? Her aunt was a wonderful person, but she was also very secretive. Obviously, Geneva never realized just how secretive.

"I don't know what is more surprising, the fact that my aunt left me so much money or the fact that I have a sister. Where did my aunt get all of this money? Who is my sister? Where is she? Why isn't she here at the reading?"

"I understand. It's all a bit overwhelming. The young lady in question — your half sister —the two of you share the same mother. Apparently, your mother had another child twenty years before you were born. Your mother lost custody of the child to the state. Your half-sister's name is Joanna Quinn. She's fifty-five years old, single and lives here in Chicago. I've been in contact with her, and she knows about the insurance policy." Nicholson slid a piece of paper across his desk to Geneva. "This is her address and telephone number. I told her about you. Your aunt's instructions were to provide you with her contact information and not vice versa. Your aunt also did not want her at the will reading. Also, there's no legal reason for her to be here. Victoria wanted you to initiate contact with Ms. Quinn at your convenience."

Geneva picked up the paper with her sister's contact information on it. She looked at it and then looked back at Mr. Nicholson.

"Why am I just now finding out about her? Why did my aunt keep her existence a secret from me for all of these years?"

Mr. Nicholson leaned back in his chair and crossed his hands.

"I'm afraid that I can't answer those questions. I only found out about your sister a few months ago when your aunt last updated her will and changed her insurance information. I've not even met Ms. Quinn. I've only spoken with her once on the telephone. With respect to your inheritance, because your aunt added you to her accounts before her death, you will have access to the funds a week from now. Do you have any additional questions?"

"Do you know where the money came from? My aunt earned a good salary at International House but certainly not enough to save ten million," Geneva said.

"I don't know all of the details, but I do know that your aunt invested in the stock market and that she was very successful at it. So I would assume that she made the money from investments. But I'm afraid that I don't know anymore than what I've told you. I only handled legal matters for her and not financial matters. I need you to sign some forms." Nicholson turned the forms on his desk so that the signature line faced Geneva. He handed her a pen. "Please sign where the signature stickers are located." Geneva signed the forms.

"There's one last thing. Your aunt wanted you to have this envelope," Nicholson said as he handed Geneva a letter sized yellow envelope. "I don't know what's in it. You'll notice that it's sealed and your aunt's signature is written across the envelope's flap."

Geneva opened the envelope. The envelope contained a safety deposit box key and the location of the box.

"This completes everything. Is there anything else that I can do for you?" Nicholson asked.

Geneva stood. "No, thank you. I guess that's it."

Mr. Nicholson stood and walked from behind his desk.

"If there's anything that you need, please don't hesitate to call me." After the two of them shook hands, he walked her out of his office and to the elevator.

# CHAPTER 11

Because Geneva had to attend the reading of her aunt's will, Zain volunteered to drop off the music CD that Victoria wanted to have played at her funeral. Zain always knew that Victoria Franklin was a woman who knew exactly what she wanted. She was not surprised that Victoria had left detailed instructions regarding her funeral and burial arrangements. One of those details involved not having anyone sing or play a musical instrument at her funeral. Instead, Victoria only wanted one of Johann Sebastian Bach's most sublime and profound organ compositions, *Toccata & Fugue in d minor*, played.

Before she left this morning, she called the business office at Rockefeller Chapel and spoke to the chapel's receptionist. Zain was surprised to learn that Su-Young Chang, a fellow I-House resident, worked at the chapel. Su provided her with a meeting time and place. Zain followed Su's meeting instructions by heading directly downstairs to the basement when she arrived at the chapel. The stone stairs to the basement ended on the right side of the hallway. In the middle of the hallway, she saw a set of stained glass double doors with a sign next to them on the wall that read, "Reception Hall." The door on the right side was open. Zain walked up to the entrance of the reception hall.

When she looked inside of the room, Margaret Kirkwood dressed in black from head to toe was putting place settings on the round tables in the room. Margaret's black attire made the paleness of her skin stand out even more. Margaret was a Ph.D. student studying

Egyptian archeology and a resident of International House. Zain stood in the doorway and watched Margaret align the placemats, plastic cutlery, paper plates, and napkins with meticulous precision as if they were fine china and crystal.

Margaret had the longest hair Zain had ever seen. Because Margaret's hair was longer than her arms and ended at her mid-calf, Zain often wondered how she managed to comb and wash it. People always knew when Margaret had sat in a chair or been in a particular room because there would be several strains of extremely long black hair left behind.

Margaret was an enigma to Zain who had started her Ph. D. program in Computer Science when Margaret started her program. However, Margaret was completing her program at a record pace. She submitted her dissertation for review in December and would probably graduate in May while Zain would only be finishing her third year.

Zain wondered if maybe Margaret's non-existent social life helped to facilitate her rapid matriculation. Margaret did not have a lot of friends. Actually, she was not sure if Margaret had any friends at all. During their first year at International House, Zain tried to become friends with her. She had long conversations with Margaret in the dining hall. But whenever she saw Margaret after each conversation, Margaret would act as if the conversations never took place. Zain finally concluded that Margaret was someone who just did not bond with other people and so Zain simply stopped engaging her socially. Whenever they passed each other, Zain would always be the one to speak first otherwise they would pass in silence. Margaret would simply walk passed her and avoid eye contact.

Zain decided to walk into the hall and to make her presence known to Margaret. But then she heard a cell phone ring and started to reach for her phone, but Margaret took her cell phone out of her skirt pocket and looked at the display.

Margaret let her phone ring four more times. Zain recalled how Margaret never picked up telephones or answered doors on the first one or two rings or knocks. Margaret believed in doing things when she was ready to do them. She waited for Margaret to finish her call.

"Will you be there Tuesday night?" Margaret asked.

"No, I'm done."

"That's the wrong answer. I expect to see you Tuesday night," Margaret continued.

Zain watched Margaret turn off her cell phone and place it back into her skirt pocket. She had almost forgotten how short Margaret could be when talking with people. After she heard Margaret's phone conversation, she was quickly reminded of Margaret's conversational style. Zain watched Margaret hold on to a chair and take a deep breath. She stepped further into the hall, made her presence known, and exchanged the customary hellos with Margaret.

"I didn't know you worked here," Zain said.

"Yes, I've worked here for the past year. I help set up for special events, and I'm also one of the carillonneurs," Margaret replied.

"What's a carillonneur?" Zain asked and immediately regretted her question.

"A carillonneur is someone who plays a carillon. It's a musical instrument consisting of twenty-three cast bronze cup-shaped bells. The carillon bells are not swung but are fixed to a metal frame. The bells themselves do not move. The clappers strike the inside lip of the bells to produce a sound. The Rockefeller Chapel carillon is the second largest instrument of its kind in the world," Margaret said.

Zain had forgotten how polymathic Margaret was. She would have to interrupt her at some point otherwise Margaret would go on and on and never ask why Zain was at the chapel in the first place. Then, Zain heard someone walking down the stone staircase. A few seconds later, Su, wearing a brown wool suit with a short skirt and black high-heeled leather boots, walked through the double doors.

"What are you two up to?" Su asked.

"Oh, we were just talking," Zain smiled as she stepped away from Margaret, and over to Su. "Those are some savage kicks that you're throwing out."

Su turned at an angle and profiled her boots with a quick curtsy.

"Thank you very much, they're Gucci, compliments of the dice."

Zain was not surprised to hear the word dice. When the fourth year Ph.D. student wasn't studying the atmospheres of the planets in the solar system, she was examining the dice, roulette and blackjack tables at the casinos in Indiana.

"Good choice as usual. How was your vacation in Seoul?" Zain asked.

"It was great. It was good to see my family again. I hadn't been home in two years."

"I'm glad to hear your trip went well."

Zain took the CD out of her purse. "Here is the CD for the funeral."

"How's Geneva doing?"

"She's ok. I suppose. She went to the reading of her aunt's will this morning," Zain replied.

"Does she have a large family?" Su asked.

"No, Victoria was Geneva's only relative," Zain replied

"If it's just the two of them, why are we setting up all of these tables?" Margaret asked.

"I'm sure Ms. Franklin had numerous friends, and I think several faculty and staff members will attend and residents too," Su said.

"Isn't it rare for someone so well liked to be murdered?" Margaret said.

"I think it was a stranger who killed her and not someone who knew her." Su said.

"Why do think that?" Zain asked.

"Well, she was so well respected and liked by so many people,"

"Sometimes that's not enough," Margaret said.

"I suppose not," Zain said. "I hate to rush, but I have to get going, ladies. I'll see you later."

She didn't mind talking to Su, but she really wanted to get away from Margaret's mouth, but more important, she wanted to be at I-House when Geneva returned from the reading of her aunt's will.

# CHAPTER 12

"Look I admit, I despised the bitch, and I certainly didn't shed any tears when she died, but I didn't kill her," Tony said as he took another slug of beer.

"You had motive, Mr. Madison. Ms. Franklin had been riding you for the past year and a half and she finally got you out of I-House and received a parting gift from your father. People have killed for far less," Yvonne said.

"I'm not people. I'm Anthony Madison the third. And I have too much to lose to go around killing people. There are other ways to get revenge. Cleaner ways."

"Revenge? Did you want revenge against Ms. Franklin?"

"Yea, I wanted revenge. And oh how easy it would've been since I live right down the street from her office and condo. I guess you've cracked the case, Sherlock."

"Where were you on the night of her death?"

"I was at The Mouliner."

"What's The Mouliner?"

"It's a private fencing club."

"You mean it's no rules sword fighting?"

"We prefer to think of it as traditional sword fighting."

"How long were you there that night?"

"I was there from nine until three in the morning. And before you ask, you can confirm that with Heather Whitmore, she runs the place. Now I really have to get back to doing more important things like drinking beer and watching wrestling."

"Do you have any trips planned?"

"No."

"Good, keep it that way."

\* \* \*

After leaving Rockefeller Chapel, Margaret took Fifty-eighth Street back to I-House. When she approached Fifty-eighth and Dorchester, she was glad she took the route because she saw Detective Peterson exit the Cloisters. She recognized the detective because she saw her interviewing people after they found Victoria's body.

Margaret's eyes moved from Detective Peterson up to a third floor window where she saw Tony Madison peeking out from behind a curtain as Detective Peterson got into in her car.

It was easy to get into the building because she entered as someone else was leaving. Margaret turned the doorknob on Tony's front door. It was not locked. She entered Tony's apartment and walked into the living room. A few minutes later he entered the room.

"What the hell are you doing here?"

"What did she want?" Margaret asked as she sat down.

"What did who want?"

"Detective Peterson. She was just here. Why?"

"She was asking me about Victoria's death."

"Did you tell her about me?"

Tony walked to the door and opened it.

"No, but if I knew that you were going to break into my apartment, I would've. Now, get out of my sight, you creepy freak."

Margaret stood up and walked toward the door, but stopped in front of Tony.

"Keep your mouth shut."

"Do you want to walk out or fly out?"

"Remember what I said."

Margaret walked into the hallway. The door slammed behind her as she continued down the hallway.

\* \* \*

Heather Whitmore sat behind her glass desk while Yvonne stood.

Yvonne was not surprised to find two walls covered in floor to ceiling mirrors in Heather's office. Ms. Whitmore seemed like someone who would want to look at her long blonde hair and pinkish skin from all angles.

"Tony was here that night. I saw him. He fenced four bouts and then spent the rest of the night watching until we closed."

"How do you know he was here the entire time?"

"I don't know but the video cameras know. We have forty digital cameras focused on the fencing area and the stands."

"I'll need to see that video."

"No problem, follow me."

Heather got up and walked across the hall from her office and into another room. The room had three walls of television monitors and a recording console in the center of the room.

"All of the recordings are stored electronically as avi files."

Heather sat down at the console and started typing on the keyboard.

"Here you go. This is the footage from that night."

Yvonne watched the video. It confirmed his alibi. He arrived at nine o'clock, fenced four bouts between ten and midnight, and then spent the rest of night, until three in the morning, watching the other bouts. Maybe Tony Madison was right, and he really did have too much to lose to kill someone.

## CHAPTER 13

Margaret was glad to be back in her room. Everything was set up for Franklin's funeral tomorrow. She was only going to attend the funeral so she could see Victoria in a casket. She had no intention of going to the burial or the gathering at Rockefeller Chapel. The last burial that she attended was her father's, and afterwards, she swore that she would never attend another burial for the rest of her life. Because she had left instructions that she not have a burial service, Margaret ensured that she would not even attend her own burial. She simply wanted to be cremated and her ashes thrown over her father's grave. She never really understood the whole burial concept. Why would people gather to see a loved one's body put into a dark, cold hole? The burial does not help the dead person, and it certainly doesn't help those left behind. Her father's burial certainly didn't help her when she was thirteen and alone.

Margaret entered her room and took off her hat, scarf, coat and boots and sat each one in her closet before she took another step into her room. She then looked at the message indicator on her phone. It was blinking and the digital display showed a number one. She pressed the message retrieval button.

"Hello, Margaret. This is your Aunt Teresa. Are you still alive? I've left you several messages, and I would appreciate it if you would return them. I want you to call me back today. I heard about the murder at International House. What is going on there? Call me back. This is not a request, Margaret."

The message ended, and Margaret hit the erase button on the machine. She was surprised her aunt did not use her usual tactic of threatening to stop her trust fund disbursements in order to get what she wanted. Margaret had no intention of calling her back. There was no reason. Victoria Franklin was dead, period. She closed the drapes in her window and walked into her closet and retrieved a wooden box. She sat the box down on her bed and opened it.

The box contained four virgin black candles, a candle lighter, and a black bottle with a label that read Wormwood oil. She picked up the bottle of oil, opened it and poured a small amount into her palm. Then she picked up one of the candles and dressed it by rubbing the oil into the candle beginning at the north end working downward to the halfway point of the candle. She continued this process with the same candle by beginning at the south end and working up to the middle.

After she dressed the other three candles, she placed them on the shelf above her bed. She picked up the candle lighter, ignited it, turned off the lights in her room and lit all four candles. After she placed the candle lighter back into the box, she stood up straight, lifted her chest, stretched out her arms with her palms turned up toward the ceiling, lifted her head back and began to chant.

"As the fire is hot
Imperium (absolute power)
As the fire burns the candle
Imperium
As the candle burns away
Imperium"

After she repeated this chant for two hours, she blew out the candles one-by-one, wrapped each one in wax paper and placed them into her garbage can.

# CHAPTER 14

By morning, the snow was hard and did not show any signs of melting away soon. Given the bitter cold, Geneva was surprised by the number of residents, staff members, and university employees who attended the funeral and the burial. Even though she never attended church regularly at the chapel or any place else, Rockefeller Chapel was the perfect place to hold the funeral because its grandness was in keeping with the essence that was Victoria Franklin.

Rockefeller Chapel was the central and dominant feature of the University of Chicago's campus. The Gothic Indiana limestone structure was set back from the street surrounded by over two acres of grassy lawn space on all four sides. When visitors arrived at the chapel, they were greeted by the Crusading Knights kneeling to the left and right above the heavy wooden doors, Michael the Archangel standing erect in the center with his sword in hand, and the angels Gabriel and Raphael stationed to the left and right of the arch springs. The inscription, "Thy Kingdom is an Everlasting Kingdom," which was carved into the limestone just above the chapel's entrance, set the stage for all who crossed the threshold.

The repast, which is the traditional gathering of family and friends that is held after a funeral in the Christian African-American community, was crowded. The reception hall in the chapel's basement hosted the repast. The hall did not compare to the vast chapel above it. Although the hall did not provide a view to the outside world, it did have windows of a fashion. A pair of double doors made of stained glass served as the room's only point of entrance and exit. The stained glass doors did not depict any particular religious scene or pattern as one would expect. But rather, they were comprised of a random arrangement of red, green, blue, and orange glass squares accompanied by a single five inch piece of clear glass in the center of each door. The hall could have been anywhere in the world. Except for the multicolored doors that led into the reception hall, the room did not contain anything to indicate that it sat beneath a thirty-two thousand ton Gothic structure.

Geneva stared at the glass doors while people chatted away at their tables but quieted down when they approached or passed by her table. Geneva and Zain sat at a rectangular table located at the back of the room directly opposite the entrance to the hall. The round tables for the guests were arranged vertically to form two rows that sat between Geneva's table and the hall's entrance. Her eyes darted around the room from table to table. She knew she should probably walk around the room and thank people for their attendance, but her feet did not move. She did not want to talk to any of them. Rather, she wanted all of them to leave. And some people even looked as if they did not want to be spoken to and would rather be someplace else.

In particular, she was thinking of Elizabeth and Bradley Wilson. Elizabeth and Bradley sat at the second table on the right hand side in front of Geneva. They sat across from each other, but they did not make eye contact with each other. The silence between them was so thick that even a jackhammer could not penetrate it.

Elizabeth Wilson was the resident manager at International House. She was a forty-five-year-old woman with two Ph.D.s who had worked at International House for over twenty years. Geneva never understood why she worked at I-House, but she often wondered if maybe it had something to do with Elizabeth's personality. During the past two years of Geneva's residency at I-House, she rarely saw Elizabeth smile, and never saw her laugh. Elizabeth was a physically attractive woman who possessed a toned body topped off by long blond hair and deep blue eyes, but her facial expression and body language could make a grown man cry, or at the very least, take cover. This was one of the reasons why she was surprised to learn today that Elizabeth was married and had a daughter. Elizabeth did not appear to be the wife and mother type. Geneva did not know that Elizabeth was married and had a child until Zain told her on the way back from the burial.

Elizabeth's husband, Bradley, who was six-feet tall with a chubby physique and thick brown hair, served as the in-house manager for the university's endowment fund. He was one of those rare men who wore bow ties instead of regular long ties and who could cry in public without shame. Bradley's face was still beet red from all of his crying at the burial. During the burial, tears streamed down Bradley's face. He made a long pause at the casket whereas his wife did not even view the body. She simply paid her respects to Geneva. Geneva decided that it would be best to leave them alone in their mutually shared silence. The decision was not a difficult one to make.

Although sporadic moments of chatter filled the room, one sound remained constant and commanded attention. This sound was the clatter of Deepa Sharma's stiletto heels hitting the tile floor. At moments, the noise generated by Deepa's heels drowned out the noise levels created by all of the various table conversations.

Deepa Sharma was a fourth year resident at the University of Chicago hospital. She moved from table to table and proudly displayed her perfect white teeth and tossed her long black hair every chance she got. Geneva over heard some of Deepa's conversation.

"Yes, we'll miss her. She was an outstanding director. She made things happen." Geneva never realized that Deepa paid attention to anything else but Deepa. Her aunt rarely talked about the residents or the staff at International House, and she certainly never mentioned Deepa's name.

When Geneva first met her two years ago, she knew that Deepa was a member of that exclusive club whose members did not have to get good grades or work hard to prove themselves. For them, acceptance by society was automatic because of their looks. Deepa was a card carrying member of this exclusive club, and she used her membership card every chance she got. Deepa's trek through the reception hall came to an end when she arrived at the Wilson table.

Geneva wondered if the silence emanating from the Wilson table propelled Deepa to skip their table all together.

The noise from the crowd started to merge into a single sound to Geneva, and she could not control the volume. It kept rising and rising in her head. She turned to Zain. "I need to get out of here."

"Are you okay? Do you need something?" Zain asked.

"I just need to be around fewer people for a while." Geneva stood and walked down the left hand side of the hall toward the double doors. She left the hall and took the stone stairs that led up to the chapel's sanctuary.

## CHAPTER 15

Inside the chapel, Geneva was small compared to the gigantic stone and concrete pillars that surrounded her. As she walked toward the pulpit, Geneva saw the intricate details of the white Appalachian oak woodcarvings that adorned the organ and south balcony. The sunlight coming through the massive mauve, amber and pale blue stained glass windows filled the chapel and illuminated their beauty. She stood in front of the pulpit with her hands in her jacket pockets. Her eyes moved from one woodcarving to the next. To her this place was beautiful, and its beauty had stood the test of time. If this chapel disappeared, the void would never be filled just like the void created by her aunt's death.

Geneva turned around and gazed at the empty chapel. The subdued color combination of the stained glass windows did not overwhelm the subtle beauty of the many sculptures and woodcarvings. Geneva walked down the center aisle and stopped in the middle of the chapel. As the daylight poured through the windows, she sat in one of the middle pews. She leaned back and stretched her legs to where her feet were in the row that was directly in front of her. She leaned her head back and looked up at the colorful tile medallions that decorated the vaulted ceiling. She closed her eyes and wondered if the past few days were all a part of a bad dream.

She felt a small hand touch her knee. Geneva opened her eyes and turned her head. Zain was sitting next to her. Geneva looked at Zain and then sat up straight on the pew. Zain put her arm around Geneva's shoulder and Geneva's head fell on Zain's shoulder.

"Do you want to cry?" Zain said while she caressed Geneva's shoulder.

Geneva lifted her head slightly and looked up at Zain. "No, I'm tired of crying. I've been crying all week. I have to stop."

"Who says that you have to stop? That's like saying you have to stop being cold when it's cold outside. If you want to cry, then cry. If you don't, then don't. But don't stop crying because you think you shouldn't cry." Zain continued to stroke Geneva's shoulder. "There's an old saying that goes, 'Man's extremity, God's opportunity' God has a plan for you, Geneva. Sometimes the road is filled with bumps and even big pots holes. But sometimes we need to hit one of the bumps or holes to remind us about who is really in charge."

Geneva lifted her head and sat up. "I know God has a plan, but sometimes I just get tired of his plan, and I want mine to work. Do you think God wants me to be alone?"

Zain turned towards Geneva. "I think everyone has felt that way at one time or another. And no, God doesn't want anyone to be alone because you're never alone. You have him. And you have me. And now, you have a sister, too." Zain embraced Geneva, and she began to cry. "Everything will be all right," Zain said.

## CHAPTER 16

Time flew by on Monday morning. One minute it was six, and then it was eight, and Geneva still had to put on her makeup to cover up the acne on her thirty-five-year-old face. Her appointment with Dr. Zimmerman was for nine. She did not like to be late or to keep people waiting. After she ate three low carb bagel snacks and drank some water, Geneva left her room. On the elevator, she remembered that she forgot to put on her makeup. She did not go back. No one cared how she looked anyway.

Dr. Omar Zimmerman's office was located in the basement of his Hyde Park townhouse. Geneva loved the old mansions in Hyde Park. She had always wanted to see the inside of his house, but she never had the nerve to ask him. She had been Dr. Zimmerman's patient since she moved into International House. This was her first visit since her aunt's death.

Each wall in his waiting room was painted to depict one of the four seasons. The summer wall was full of sunflowers, lakes, and sunsets. The autumn wall was covered in red and golden leaves, wooden bridges and mountains. The spring wall was alive with daisies, green hills and trees. The winter wall depicted snow covered trees, frozen lakes, and snow capped mountaintops.

Geneva sat with her back against the summer wall and faced the winter wall. Even though he denied it, she knew there was some sort of psychological reason why he had his waiting room decorated in this manner. She glanced at her watch and wondered why she could never time things exactly. She was always waiting because she was always early. Dr. Zimmerman kept his office expenses to a minimum. One of the ways he managed to do this was to employ a piece of framed laminated stationary to serve as his secretary. The stationary read, "Please be seated, the doctor will be with you shortly." When she arrived for her appointments, she was always alone. She never saw anyone else leaving when she arrived, or arriving when she left. Geneva thought he must have lots of patients otherwise how could he afford such an expensive home?

Like most patients in therapy, when she first met Dr. Zimmerman, Geneva had a huge crush on him. She would fantasize about him kissing her. Geneva hadn't done that in over a year.

She went into therapy because her aunt thought that it might help her deal with her feelings of low self-esteem and loneliness. Geneva was surprised when her aunt recommended that she start therapy with Dr. Zimmerman. Her aunt was a very self-reliant person. Geneva could never imagine her aunt going to a therapist or recommending someone else to go. But Geneva was glad that her aunt made the recommendation. Over the past two years, her self-esteem improved. Before she started seeing Dr. Zimmerman, she always wanted to change something about her appearance. She wanted to change her nose because it was too big, her cheeks because they were too fat, and the rest of her body from the shoulders down because she was too fat all over. She had made and cancelled so many appointments at the liposuction clinic that they stopped accepting her appointments. Learning to accept oneself is very difficult in a world that is saturated with media images of perfect, thin women with long hair.

Over the past two years, Geneva revealed things to Dr. Zimmerman that she never dreamed she would ever say out loud to another living soul. However, Dr. Zimmerman had never revealed anything about his personal life. Every time she tried to ask him something, he always said that we were here to discuss Geneva and not Omar.

But she did know that at one point in his life, he had to face his own demons. Before she started her sessions with Dr. Zimmerman, her aunt told her that he had worked in the Cook County Hospital's psychiatric unit for over twenty years until one of his patients killed a nurse and then killed himself. After the suicide of his patient, Dr. Zimmerman took a long sabbatical and joined the Peace Corps for three years. When she started her therapy with him, he had only been back in the United States for six months. She was his first new patient.

The door to Dr. Zimmerman's office opened. If Geneva had not been looking in the direction of the door, she would not have known that it was open. Dr. Zimmerman stood in the doorframe. He was a lean man with a solid head of white hair and a full white beard that seemed whiter because of his milk chocolate complexion. He smiled. "Good morning, Geneva. Come in."

Dr. Zimmerman turned and went back into his office. She barely heard him and often she wanted to yell at him to speak up. But who was she to talk; she didn't always speak up or for that matter talk.

Geneva sat in the leather chair in front of his antique wood desk. She wished that he had a couch. The bareness of Dr. Zimmerman's office did not permit distractions. The room only contained his desk, his chair, the patient's chair, a ceiling light, his notepad, and his pen. He had glass block windows, and the floor was tiled. He sat and stared at Geneva. Geneva stared back. The sessions always started the same. She never knew what he was waiting for her to do. He placed his elbows on the arms of his chair.

"I was sorry to hear about the death of your aunt. How are you feeling?" Dr. Zimmerman asked.

Her hands started to shake slightly. She was nervous, but she did not know why.

"I don't know how I feel." Geneva extended her feet in front of her. "I miss my aunt. I'm angry that someone took her away from me. I'm also confused and happy."

Dr. Zimmerman leaned forward and picked up his pen and began to write.

"You're angry, confused and happy. What do you mean?"

Geneva shifted slightly in her chair and looked down at his desk.

"I'm angry at myself. Someone killed my only living relative, and I'm consumed by the fact that I'm alone rather than the fact that she is dead and someone killed her. I'm being selfish and I know it. But I don't know how to stop it. During my aunt's will reading, I found out that I have a large sum of money and a half sister."

"How do you feel about having a large sum of money and a half-sister?" Dr. Zimmerman asked.

"I'm excited and scared. I hope that I don't waste the money. I always wanted a sister. But she's twenty years older than me, and she may not like me. We might hate each other. I desperately want us to get along. See what I mean, I'm thinking about myself and my aunt has been murdered."

"You were lonely before your aunt died. Now your loneliness is more intensified and maybe even more obvious to you. The fact that you acknowledge your loneliness does not mean that you are being selfish. Also, you have a new relative who might relieve some of your loneliness. You have a large amount of money to manage. You are thinking about all of these things. You're not being selfish by thinking about what you want and what you need. How did you feel about your aunt?"

"I admired and respected her. I was grateful to her as well. She made a success of her life. She did not let anything or anyone get in her way. She was always supportive of me. My aunt put me through college and graduate school. She was more of a mother to me than my own mother. I loved her, and I know she loved me. I often wished I could be like her. I'm always making the wrong decision. She always appeared to make the correct decision. My aunt Victoria always knew what to do in any situation."

Dr. Zimmerman stopped writing and laid his pen down on his desk, leaned forward on his desk and interlocked his hands.

"We all make mistakes. Mistakes help us to learn, if we are paying attention to the mistakes. Have you repeated any of your mistakes?"

Geneva looked down at his desk and around the room. She desperately wished that he had something on his walls.

"I don't think I have repeated my mistakes. But I just want to stop making them."

"Human beings will never stop making mistakes. That is part of what makes us human. Making mistakes is a part of the process of becoming a better person."

"I hate the process," Geneva said.

"Hating it is the wrong approach. Figuring out a way to manage it is a better alternative."

Dr. Zimmerman continued the session for another forty-five minutes during which time he gave suggestions about how to manage mistakes and to let go of the guilt one feels after making a mistake. When the little red light on his desk clock started to blink, Dr. Zimmerman stood and walked from behind his desk.

"Well, our time is up. I want you to think about how you can manage the fact that you will always make mistakes."

Geneva stood and headed towards the door as Dr. Zimmerman came towards her. "Thank you, I'll see you next week," Geneva said.

Geneva did not always understand Dr. Zimmerman's line of thinking. But it was good for her to talk to someone about the things on her mind. Sometimes she talked to Zain, but Zain could not relate to her feelings. Zain came from a large family and even though they were spread between Jamaica, Cuba and the U.S., she talked to them often. It was hard for Geneva to describe her feelings of loneliness and sometimes anger to Zain. This was why she saw Dr. Zimmerman.

# CHAPTER 17

After leaving Dr. Zimmerman's office, Geneva decided to go to her aunt's bank and open the safety deposit box. She did not have to go back to I-House to get the key because it was still in her purse from when she attended the reading of her aunt's will.

Geneva only had to show her driver's license and the deposit key in order to obtain access to the safety deposit box area. A clerk escorted her into the vault and once inside the vault, the clerk pulled out the box and carried it into another windowless room. The clerk placed the metal box on the table and left the room.

She sat in front of the box and stared at it. She then took the key out of her purse and opened the box. The box contained a sealed letter-size white envelope. Geneva opened the envelope, removed the piece of paper and unfolded it. The paper was a sheet of Victoria's personal stationary. The stationary was handwritten and addressed to Geneva and contained only the names of two banks, the accounts held at each institution, and the online user Ids and passwords for the banks.

Geneva placed the piece of stationary in her purse and relocked the box. She did not know why her aunt had left her the account information especially since according to Mr. Nicholson she would have access to the accounts next week.

\* \* \*

Zain arrived thirty minutes early at the Center for East Asian Studies because she wanted to be sure to get a good seat to see the movie. She had never been to the center before so she did not know what to expect with respect to the seating accommodations. When she arrived, she was glad she came early.

The Center for East Asian Studies consisted of a large sitting area surrounded by five offices on two sides. The sitting area had a fifty-two-inch wide screen television and two couches with a table behind one of the couches. The table contained various East Asian oriented magazines.

Zain claimed her seat on the couch that gave her a direct view of the television. She always wanted to see the film, "The Five Fingers of Death," but she had zero success trying to order it online. The film was the first international martial arts movie to become a box office hit, and as a result, it launched the Kung Fu movie craze during the 1970s in the United States.

After reading a magazine in the sitting area for fifteen minutes, the door leading into the center opened, and Su entered the room. Wearing a pair of blood red three-inch heeled boots, Su sauntered her petite, 38D bouncing frame over to the second couch, sat down and pulled out an issue of Vanity Fair.

"Do you come here often to see movies?" Su asked.

"No. This is my first time here. I've always wanted to see this film. I'm a big Kung Fu movie fan," Zain replied.

"I come here every week to see a film. I like anything that's free."

"How's Geneva doing? I haven't seen her lately."

"She's doing as well as can be expected," Zain replied.

"That's good. Tell me, does Xavier still conduct his poetry workshop at I-House?" Su asked.

"Yes, he does."

"Has Geneva made any moves?"

"What are you talking about?"

"You know what I'm talking about. Geneva is interested in him. Isn't that why she joined the workshop?"

"No, she hasn't done anything," Zain replied.

"Well, she should. She would be way better for him than Deepa."

"Deepa? Did they used to date?"

"Yes, they dated until she dumped him. I used to see them together at various restaurants and walking around Hyde Park together. After they broke up, he was depressed. I think he started drinking," Su said.

"It's unfortunate that he got hurt. But it doesn't surprise me. Deepa is not the most pleasant person on the planet. He's probably better off without her," Zain said.

"Do you see any tension between the two of them since they both still live at I-House?" Su asked.

"I really don't know. I rarely see either one of them," Zain said. The door leading into the center opened again and two other Chinese women entered the room followed by a Japanese man.

"I was just wondering," Su said.

Zain was glad the other three people entered the room because it meant that Su would stop talking about Xavier and Deepa. She was correct. Su opened up her magazine and started reading.

The Japanese man turned on the television and put in the DVD of the movie. He checked the time on his watch and looked at the clock on the wall above the television set.

He started the movie. Zain was not surprised to find out that Xavier and Deepa used to date. Men have always been interested in women who look like Deepa. The exotic cover always pulled them in. Later on, the contents between the covers got them into trouble. More often than not, when men have to make a choice between enjoying sex with a beautiful woman who has a sour disposition and selfish tendencies, and another woman who may not be as beautiful but who is kind and thoughtful, they always choose the former and they always regret it later.

# CHAPTER 18

As Geneva approached the Home Room in International House on Monday night, she knew she did not want to attend her weekly poetry workshop even though it meant she would have the pleasure of Xavier's smile and voice. Xavier Lakemore led the weekly workshop. And in fact, the only reason that she joined the workshop was to meet and be around Xavier. Xavier was born to a British father and an African American mother. He grew up in London and was Oxford trained. Xavier was six feet of exemplary British manners and keen intellect who possessed the most beautiful soft brown eyes she had ever seen.

When Geneva arrived, Xavier was sitting at the head of the table. Charles Templeton and Barbara Miller were seated in the middle opposite each other. Geneva sat next to Barbara. She sent Xavier an email message about her aunt. Xavier, Charles and Barbara were all unable to attend the funeral services, but they each sent their condolences in the form of cards.

Geneva always looked forward to attending the workshop because it made her feel like a real writer, and she got to see Xavier. She enjoyed hearing Xavier's Oxford educated British accent and seeing the straight white set of teeth that made up his smile. Usually, she could listen to his voice and look at his smile for hours and not think about anything else, but tonight it was different. Geneva's mind wandered to thoughts about her newly found sister, Joanna. Geneva needed to call her tomorrow to set up their first meeting. She put off making the call because she could not decide if they should meet at International House, another public place, or Joanna's home. Her claustrophobic room was not an option. Finally, she decided it was probably best for the two of them to meet for breakfast at the Pancake House on Fifty-first Street in Hyde Park.

Charles sneezed and Geneva was reminded of her surroundings. She clasped the submissions in both hands as she looked at the pages. Because poetry is meant to be heard, and not necessarily read, everyone was supposed to bring multiple copies of their poems for the critique session. One copy would serve as the sacrifice and be slashed by the red pen and the other copy was for the participants so they could read along as the author read his or her respective poem out loud.

"I think we should do something different tonight. Instead of going through the critiques, let's just read one of the poems out loud and then all of us write down what we think about the selected poem. And next week, we will reread it and see if we feel the same way," Xavier said as he sat up straight in his chair and folded his hands on the table.

"Geneva, could you please read your poem for us tonight?" Xavier asked.

"Ok," Geneva said, as she shuffled through the pages in front of her. She wanted to say no, but she knew Charles and Barbara did not want to read. So, there was no point in putting them in that position.

She held the poem entitled, *Enigma*, with both hands and began to read.

"Is loneliness not knowing who to talk to in a crowded room?
Is loneliness not knowing who will hold your hand?
Is loneliness not knowing who will hug you?
Is loneliness not knowing who will kiss you?
Is loneliness not knowing who will miss you?
Is loneliness not knowing who will call you?
Is loneliness not knowing who will remember you?
Or is loneliness just living every day?"

After she finished reading, everyone started writing their impressions. She looked at the wall clock directly behind Xavier. An hour had elapsed; it was eight-thirty. Xavier looked at Geneva, and then in the direction of the window behind Barbara and then collected the papers in front of him.

"Well, it appears to be snowing rather heavily outside. Let's end early so those of us who don't have the pleasure of living at International House have a shorter travel time home," Xavier said.

After Xavier had adjourned the workshop, Charles was the first to leave the room and Barbara soon followed him. Geneva wanted to be the first to leave, but she did not want to be too obvious about it. As a result, she and Xavier were the last to leave.

"Would you like to have dinner with me tonight?" Xavier asked.

Geneva wanted to say yes. How often had she fantasized about Xavier asking her to go anyplace with him? But, tonight, her rejection of his offer came out of her mouth before she even realized it.

"No, thank you. I actually have a headache. I'm just going to go to bed early tonight."

"Oh, I'm sorry to hear that you aren't feeling well. Maybe some other time," Xavier said.

The two of them finished collecting their belongings. Xavier turned off the lights and they left the room. Geneva used Xavier's need to return the key to the front desk as an exit point. She regretted that she had to decline his invitation. But at the moment, she really did not want to think about him anymore than she already did. And if she had dinner with him, she knew that he would occupy her thoughts way more than he probably should.

# CHAPTER 19

Geneva was surprised that she was able to get up at six in the morning and feel well rested. She could not remember the last time she had a good night's sleep. Last night, she managed to sleep through the night.

After she finished her breakfast in the dining hall, Geneva returned to her room. The Tuesday morning sunshine poured through the window. She stood in front of the window and gazed out at the fresh batch of snow that fell during the night. The undisturbed snow sat on the Midway and the sidewalks around International House. She had an entire day to do some writing and some chores. As she turned around, she heard a knock at her door.

"Come in," Geneva said.

The door opened and Elizabeth Wilson stepped into her room.

"Hello, Elizabeth," Geneva said surprised.

"I hope it's not too early to be visiting you, but I need to ask you to do something," Elizabeth said.

Because Elizabeth was never one to waste time with the customary social pleasantries, Geneva was surprised she expressed doubt about the timing of her visit. Elizabeth always got to the point in her conversations. Some people thought her conversational style was rather cold especially since Elizabeth's interactions with other people were rarely accompanied by a smile. But, Geneva liked it. Direct questions accompanied by brevity, Geneva believed, warranted respect whereas longwinded social phrases did not.

"What do you need me to do?" Geneva asked.

"I need you to return your aunt's laptop and her office and building keys to me. They are probably in her condo at The Nobel House. Can you bring the laptop and keys to me?"

Elizabeth's request made Geneva, for the first time, think about the fact that she had to go to her aunt's condo and pack up her belongings. In fact, because she inherited the condo, she would probably be moving into it. But, she was not in a hurry to go through her aunt's things or to move.

"Sure, I can get them for you. Is next week okay?" Geneva asked.

"The laptop and the keys belong to International House and the university. I need to get them back no later than tomorrow," Elizabeth said.

"I see. Then, I will bring them by your office tomorrow before you go home."

"I have a repair man coming to the house tomorrow. So I will be working from home. I don't want the laptop and especially the keys to be lying around the office. Things have a habit of growing legs. Do you know where I live on Kimbark?"

Geneva knew where Elizabeth lived because one day during the summer her aunt had pointed out the house to her.

"I will bring the laptop and the keys by your house tomorrow," Geneva said.

"Good, " Elizabeth said, turning on her heels to leave.

Because she did not want to go to her aunt's condo so soon, and she certainly did not want to go alone, she decided to ask Zain to go with her to retrieve the laptop and the keys.

Secretly, she wanted Zain to go alone to the condo, but Geneva knew that it would really be unfair to ask Zain to do such a thing. After all, Victoria was her aunt, and it was her responsibility to manage her aunt's estate and this included tidying up any loose ends.

\* \* \*

Zain agreed to accompany Geneva to Victoria's condo. Victoria's condo was in the Nobel House, which was directly in back of International House on Dorchester. The building was commonly referred to as the Nobel House because during the past thirty years, several Nobel Prize winners from the University of Chicago had lived in the building. The contemporary style fifteen-story building contained only full floor condominium units. Victoria's unit was on the sixth floor.

When Geneva entered the condo, closely followed by Zain, she immediately noticed that the aroma of fresh flowers that used to greet her whenever she visited her aunt's house had been replaced by the stench of dirty water. The flowers on the table in the foyer were dead and the water in the glass vase had become murky with black particles swimming around in it. Geneva walked into the living room, which provided a western view of the university campus and Washington Park. The flowers on the cocktail table were dead, and the plants around the windows were wilted and starved for water. The sunshine pouring through the windows illuminated the dust blanket that covered the black baby grand piano in the southern corner of the room. Geneva did not know how many times she had visited her aunt's house. But this was the first time that she had ever seen dust anywhere in her aunt's house.

Geneva put her hands in her coat pockets and walked into the dining room and then the kitchen. She opened the doors to the two spare bedrooms but did not walk into them. The double doors to her aunt's bedroom were wide open. Rather than enter the room, Geneva and Zain stood in the doorway. The brass canopy bed was neatly made as usual but like the previous rooms in the condo, the flowers on the nightstand were dead.

"It doesn't look like the laptop is here but maybe the keys are," Zain said as she stepped passed Geneva and began to enter the master bedroom.

Geneva grabbed Zain's arm and stopped her. "You're right, the laptop is not here. It's probably in her study and the keys are probably there, too."

"The keys could be here. Let's just take a quick look around and see," Zain said.

"No, I don't want to look in here. Let's just go to the study and look for the keys and the laptop there," Geneva said.

Zain did not respond. She simply followed Geneva into Victoria's study. The study contained a south facing window that provided a perfect view of the parking lot behind I-House. The walls on the left and right side of the room contained floor-to-ceiling bookshelves. From the doorway, she immediately saw the laptop on Victoria's desk. Geneva slowly walked into the room and went directly to the claw footed oak desk that sat directly in front of the window.

She packed the laptop and then started looking for the keys. She did not have to look long. They were in the top drawer on the right side of the desk. The key ring contained nine keys with adhesive labels that read office, front door, back door, side doors, office master, common rm master, basement master, files, and room master. Except for the key labeled room master, all of the keys had a square top with the university crest on it. The room master key not only contained the crest but it also contained four holes, one in each corner of the key's square top.

"Did you know there was a master key for all of the rooms in I-House, the common rooms, and the rooms in the basement," Geneva asked.

"No, I didn't know that. No, wonder Elizabeth was so adamant about getting them back as soon as possible. Although, I still think she could have shown you a little consideration," Zain said.

"She's just someone who doesn't like to beat around the bush about things, and she asks for things when she wants them. She's assertive," Geneva said.

"Assertive is a useful adjective but so is arrogant," Zain said.

"Let's get out of here; we have what we came for."

"When are you going to take the stuff to her?" Zain asked.

"Tomorrow morning," Geneva said.

Geneva and Zain left the study and walked back to the foyer. When Geneva opened the front door to leave, her cell phone rang. She took the phone out of her coat pocket and answered it.

"No problem, I can come by tomorrow morning. I will be there at nine," Geneva said.

"Who was that?" Zain asked.

"It was Detective Peterson. She wants to talk to me tomorrow morning. So I guess Elizabeth will have to wait until after I get through with Detective Peterson."

"What does she want to talk to you about?"

"I don't know. She didn't say. She just said that she had some follow-up questions for me," Geneva said.

Geneva and Zain left the condo. On the elevator, Geneva wondered if she should have thrown out the dead flowers, but she realized that it did not matter because they would not be replaced so they could sit a little longer.

# CHAPTER 20

Zain stood in the door way as Heather shook hands with Sean Fielding, a freshman at the university. She stepped into the studio and made her presence known.

"What's going on?" Zain asked.

"Why nothing dear. Sean and I were just finishing up," Heather said as she reached into her purse and pulled out a business card. "Here's my card, call me anytime," she continued as she handed Sean the card.

Sean said goodbye to both of them and left the studio.

"What's wrong with you? That kid is only 18 years old. He doesn't need to be at The Mouliner."

"I think that's for him to decide and not you. Not everyone backs down like you."

"I don't back down. I practice caution."

"Really, let's see, shall we." Heather walked over to the weapon stand. She took off her coat and along with her purse laid them both down on the floor. Then she picked up a sabre, tossed it to Zain and then removed another one for herself.

"On guard," Heather cried.

Immediately the two swords began to dance and glitter as the afternoon sun beamed through the studio's windows and the combat began with the natural animosity that exists between a bully and a target.

With every step of her advance toward Heather, Zain's heart rate increased and sweat occupied her forehead. Heather fought on the defensive and executed a vigorous side thrust and sent Zain's sword out of her hand and into the air.

Zain took two steps backward, but her foot slipped and she fell on to her back. Heather lunged forward and said to Zain, pointing her sword to her throat, "I guess, I win."

Zain heard the studio's door open and close. "Hey, what's going on in here?" Xavier yelled.

Heather removed the point of her sword from Zain's throat. Xavier ran into the studio.

"What the hell are you two doing?"

"Oh we were just playing. Isn't that right, Zain?"

Xavier looked down at Zain and then squatted down next to her.

"Are you alright? Are you hurt?"

Zain stared at him. She didn't know what to say.

"Zain are you alright?" Xavier asked.

"Yea, I'm ok," she said as she started to sit up. Xavier stood up and extended his hand to help her up from the floor.

"Well, it's been peachy, but I must be going," Heather said as she walked over to the sword rack and placed her saber in it.

"Heather, you know that you're not supposed to be here, and you certainly are not supposed to be free form fencing here, either."

"And, I missed you too," Heather said smiling.

"I don't want to see anymore stunts like this again or I'll have you arrested. Do you understand me?"

"We'll see," Heather said as she walked out of the studio.

Xavier stood in front of Zain with his hands on his waist.

"What is wrong with you? Are you crazy? You never free form fence especially with someone like Heather," Xavier said.

"You're right. I wasn't thinking. She made me angry," Zain replied.

"That's the point. You never free form fence when you're angry. You endanger your life and someone else's. Why were the two of you fighting?"

"It's a long story."

"I have time. How do you know her? She left the fencing club before you came here."

"We went to high school together. She comes from a wealthy family. They own three of the largest resorts in Montego Bay. She made high school miserable for me. I was her amusement for three years. She's the reason I graduated early. I wanted to get away from her. We were on the fencing team together, and she never lost."

"And obviously, nothing has changed."

"Obviously, but it can if you help me."

"What do you mean, help you?"

"I want you to help me to train for The Mouliner. I want to beat Heather on her own turf."

"Revenge never helps anyone. Walking away is the better option. Fighting her won't make you feel any better and it won't undo all the things that she did to you."

"I want to find out. Will you help me?"

"No, I won't. I won't help you to hurt yourself or someone else, not even Heather."

# CHAPTER 21

Using the side entrance on the east side of the building, Margaret entered Rockefeller Chapel that night. She walked down the east aisle to the front of the chapel and peeked through the window at the top of the sanctuary's side door. As usual, the security guard was fast asleep. She turned around and walked to the back of the sanctuary. She went behind the pipe organ and pulled on a metal knob. Part of the wood paneled wall behind the organ opened to reveal a long steep staircase. She pulled out a flashlight from the left pocket of her coat. Holding the banister with her right hand and the flashlight with her left, she walked down the steep flight of stairs. The stairs ended at another door. Margaret unlocked the door and stepped into a small room. The room had a stone floor, stone walls, a small bench and a second door. She sat the flashlight on the bench with the light beaming up toward the ceiling. She took off her clothes and placed them neatly folded on the floor next to the bench. She then bent over and pulled out a long black hooded robe from underneath the bench and put it on.

She put the hood over her head and opened the second door in the room. She lifted a metal lever on the wall next to the door and eight kerosene lanterns were ignited. The light from the lanterns revealed a large square room with stone walls and a stone floor. The floor contained a large black circle with a pentacle drawn in its center. In its center, the pentacle contained a long rectangular table covered with a red satin cloth.

The table served as an altar during Margaret's *Words of Power* rituals. After she finished her second year of graduate school, she discovered the sheets of papyrus that contained the *Words of Power* when she was in Egypt for the summer. The Egyptian goddess Isis used the *Words of Power* to compel people and things to fulfill her requests. Isis uttered words that drove the poison out of Ra's limbs, that restored her husband to life, and that restored her son to life after he was stung by a scorpion.

Margaret walked over to the altar and stood in front of it. Two other individuals entered the room wearing black robes. They entered the room with their arms crossed and their heads down. They stood directly behind Margaret as she bent over and placed her arms underneath the satin cloth and pulled out a wooden box. The wooden box had another small black narrow case on top of it. She sat the box on top of the altar, placed the narrow case on the side of the box, and then opened the box.

One-by-one she removed five virgin black candles and handed two candles to each of the individuals behind her. She kept the fifth candle, and using a candle lighter, she lit it and used it to light the other four candles. They placed one candle at each point of the pentacle on the floor and then returned to their positions in front of the altar.

After she lit the candles, she took out a black granite bowl and placed it on the altar. Then she took out a wooden spoon and sat it next to the granite bowl. She reached her hand back into the wooden box and pulled out a small jar labeled black cat's blood and poured half of the jar into the bowl. Next, she took out another small jar labeled snake ashes and poured half of it into the bowl. Finally, she removed a ball of blonde hair that belonged to her father and placed the hair in the bowl. She picked up the spoon and mixed the contents in the bowl together. She put the spoon back into the box and closed it. After she closed the wooden box, she opened the narrow case and removed a dagger containing a golden handle carved in the image of a snake and sat it in front of the granite bowl.

She put the dagger case back on top of the wooden box and placed them under the altar. She pulled out a black leather book and opened it. The book held loose sheets of papyrus, which contained the *Words of Power*. With both hands, she lifted up the granite bowl and began to read and the other two people repeated after her.

"Black spirits and white,
Red spirits and grey,
Harken to me I say.
Five points of the Circle, weave the spell,
Red is for break of day,
White is for the noon tide hour,
Grey is for twilight
Black is for the place of power
Great ones, spirits from the past,
Witness it and guard it fast."

Then she lifted the dagger and they repeated the same chant. The other two people continued to stand with their arms folded and their heads bowed. After she sat the dagger on the altar directly in front of the granite bowl, she stretched out her arms with her palms turned up toward the ceiling and began to read.

"There has been unfairness done to me
I summon the elements
I invoke them
I conjure them to do my bidding
There shall be fear and bad blood
There shall be submission and no mercy
I point the Words of Power against thee
A hundred fold is the cost for my anger and pain
Thee shall be blinded by fear
Blinded by pain
Blinded by me
Cursed by me
So it must be!"

Margaret lowered her arms, walked to each point on the pentacle and blew out each candle.

# CHAPTER 22

Every time she entered Captain Ingram's office, she knew it involved the progression of his career. The murder of Victoria Franklin was a high profile case, and he wanted to look good and looking good depended on an arrest being made. Peterson entered Ingram's office and decided to stand even after he asked her to sit down.

"How close are we to making an arrest?" Ingram asked.

"Not very close at all. But, I think someone else may have died in preparation for Franklin's murder," Peterson replied.

"So a practice murder was committed?"

"Not quite but sort of, Franklin's toxicology report revealed that she was injected with a neuromuscular blocking agent called norcuron and hexachorophane that causes blindness. They would have caused her to be completely immobilized, mute and blind. Norcuron was found in Devon Bannister after he died."

"Was he stabbed to death?"

"No, he died from an asthma attack. But, I think the killer needed to see how much of the neuromuscular agent he or she would need to work on someone Franklin's height and weight. Bannister and Franklin were the same height and weight. The practice immobilization went wrong and Bannister suffered an asthma attack and the person who injected him left him to die."

"Have you found any other connections besides the drug?"

"No, that's it. I've talked to Bannister's grandmother, the hotel clerk and a woman who may have been his girlfriend. And the people who knew Franklin did not know him."

"It just might be a coincidence. I think you should question Franklin's niece again. She didn't have an alibi," said Ingram.

"But there's no evidence linking her to the crime," replied Peterson.

"But there are ten million motives."

"She was her aunt's only heir. But that doesn't make her a murderer."

"Bring her in for questioning."

"There is no need to bring her down here."

"I'm not asking."

The phone rang and he picked it up.

"Yes, chief. We're progressing on the Franklin case. The lead detective, Peterson, is going to question the niece again. We think she has the strongest motive," Ingram said as he waved Peterson out his office. She turned and left. She held on to the doorknob and hesitated for moment because she wanted to slam it shut but had second thoughts and decided not to.

## CHAPTER 23

The dingy walls of the interview room at the police station made the room's grey tile appear cleaner than it was. Geneva had only been in the room for ten minutes, but the cushioned folding chair already hurt her buttocks. Detective Peterson entered the room and sat in front of Geneva.

"Thank you for coming down," Detective Peterson said.

"No, problem. Have there been any developments in the case?" Geneva asked.

"Not really. However, I have some questions for you. Do you mine if I record this conversation?" Detective Peterson said.

"No, I don't mind. What do you need to know?"

"We just need to clear up a few things." Detective Peterson turned on the recorder. "Today is Wednesday, January 19, 2005, and the time is nine-fifteen a.m. I am Detective Yvonne Peterson interviewing Geneva Anderson in interview room number two." Detective Peterson leaned forward on the table. "Geneva, did you know prior to her death that your aunt had an estate worth ten million dollars?"

"No, I didn't know anything about my aunt's estate. Like I said, she never discussed her financial affairs with me," Geneva replied.

"Do you know how your aunt got ten million dollars?" Detective Peterson asked.

"No, I don't. She was always telling me about the need to invest my money. She knew a lot about the stock market. She was always buying and selling stock. I think she made it through investments. But, I honestly don't know how she made her money."

"You mean you never wondered how your aunt could afford to put you through school and live in a condo at the Nobel House?" Detective Peterson asked.

"Well, there were times when I asked her how she could afford to put me through school. But she always just told me not to worry about it. She used to say that being able to help people is one reason to save your money and that one day I might have to do the same for someone."

"Is it correct that you received access to your aunt's bank accounts today?"

"Yes, that's correct," Geneva replied.

"Geneva, can anyone confirm that you were in your room on Monday night between eleven and one in the morning?"

"No. I didn't talk to anyone that night. Why do I need someone to confirm my whereabouts? What are you implying?"

"Geneva, you're a bright woman. And you have a lot of years ahead of you. Your life does not have to be over," Detective Peterson said in gentle voice.

"What do you mean, my life doesn't have to be over?" Geneva did not appreciate Peterson's condensing tone. She was a suspect because of her aunt's generosity and maybe even her secrecy.

"Geneva, if something happened between you and your aunt, now is the time to tell me. I can help you," Detective Peterson said.

"Nothing happened between me and my aunt. There's nothing to tell. If you think I killed my aunt, then you're wrong. I had nothing to do with my aunt's death."

"You have to admit that it looks suspicious. You're Victoria's sole beneficiary, and you don't have an alibi for Monday. There are no other suspects."

"I don't care how it looks. I didn't know about my aunt's will. I did not kill my aunt. Are you arresting me?"

"No, we're not arresting you. But don't take any long trips." Detective Peterson concluded the interview and Geneva left the room.

Geneva walked out of the police station and down the street. After walking three blocks away from the station, she looked around but did not see her car. She realized that she had passed her car. She turned around and walked back two blocks towards the police station. She got into her car and took off her glasses to wipe away her tears. Because of her aunt's generosity, she was now a murder suspect. Geneva did not know where the money really came from. Her aunt Victoria was very kind, but she was also very secretive.

# CHAPTER 24

The broken sheets of ice extended as far as Peterson's eye could see across Lake Michigan. From her mother's window, she gazed out at the frozen waters of the city's great lake. Wilma Peterson lived on the top floor of the Montgomery House Assisted Living facility. As she stood and admired the view from her mother's living room window, she remembered how her mother delayed her move into the facility for two years so she could get a unit on the top floor. Her mother did not wait that long because of the unit's quality or the view that it provided but simply because she did not like to have people walking on top of her head.

Detective Peterson knew all to well that once her mother set her mind on something not even wild horses could make her change direction. After all, her mother had gone to great lengths to try and get her only daughter married off.

"I'm glad that you came by. Your timing is perfect," Mrs. Peterson said as she walked into the living room and sat down. "You know you're old when you sit down and it hurts," she continued.

"Is your arthritis bad today?"

"Yes, but it's bad everyday. It's just some days it likes to be assertive. But I showed it who's boss in this house. I walked the perimeter of the first floor today."

Wilma Peterson was a chubby, petite, seventy-two-year-old woman with short salt and pepper hair. For the past seven years, she has suffered with arthritis in her legs. And Detective Peterson could count the number of times her mother complained on one hand.

"Sit down. Enjoy it now while you still can. I never thought I would miss the relief provided by a good chair."

Detective Peterson sat as her mother asked her.

"Tyler Nelson came by today to visit his mother. We had a wonderful conversation. You should meet him. He'll be here on Sunday."

"We'll see. Do you want to go out to dinner on Sunday?"

"Yes, that would be great. We can invite Mrs. Nelson and Tyler. He's an only child, too, and he's never been married."

"Yes, you told me all of this before. I don't think I'm going to be in the mood to socialize on Sunday."

"Today is Wednesday. How do you know what mood you'll be in on Sunday? You shouldn't predict doom before it happens. What are you doing tonight?"

"Why? Did you want to do something?"

"No, I just wanted to know if you were going to be home tonight."

"Why mom? What are you up to?"

"Nothing. I'm not up to anything except trying to get my stubborn daughter a husband. How many suitable men have you passed up? I have lost count."

"I find that hard to believe."

"You're right. I do know. The total is one hundred and seventeen. You have no idea how much hard work I have to do. If you did, you wouldn't be so cavalier."

"Yes, mom. I know."

"No, you don't know. Do you think it's easy talking to all of these old people day after day about their sons, nephews, and grandsons? I have to hear about their aches, doctors, appetites, medications, churches, and hairdressers day after day after day. It's hard work. And you don't appreciate it."

"I do appreciate it really. Do you want me to massage your feet?"

Mrs. Peterson reclined her chair and lifted her feet as the footrest came out. Yvonne placed one of the ottomans in front her mother's chair and began to massage her feet.

# CHAPTER 25

Elizabeth and Bradley Wilson lived one block from International House on Fifty-eighth and Kimbark. Their house was one of several wood framed Victorian homes that sat on the quiet one-way street across from the Metra train tracks. That afternoon, Geneva walked up the stairs to the front door and heard faint arguing. As she was about to ring the bell, she noticed that the front door was not closed completely but rather just pushed up.

The windows on both sides of the door revealed that no one was in the foyer. She looked into the living room's large picture window and did not see anyone. After she turned around and scanned the street, she gently opened the front door and entered the house. When she entered the foyer, she could easily hear Elizabeth and Bradley's voices coming from the back of the house and from what appeared to be the kitchen. Geneva stood in the foyer and listened.

"Elizabeth, will you please, for the love of God, leave me alone," Bradley said.

"I can't believe you have the nerve to use the words 'love' and 'God' in the same breath. You are the last person who should be using those two words together," Elizabeth said.

"I have a lot on my mind. I would like to spend a quiet day at home and not listen to a screaming wife," Bradley said.

"Home? You don't live here. You just pass through to eat, sleep, and change your suits," Elizabeth said.

"Maybe there's nothing here," Bradley said frowning.

"You make me sick. You're a pathetic excuse for a man. That's why your mistress didn't want you anymore. She woke up and saw you for the sorry excuse that you are."

Geneva heard a door slam.

"Just like a coward to leave when the going gets a little tough," Elizabeth said.

Geneva turned around and went back outside and closed the door behind her. She stood on the porch and waited a few minutes. And then she rang the bell. Elizabeth came to the door.

"Good, you have the laptop," Elizabeth said. Elizabeth reached for the laptop and Geneva handed it to her.

"Yes, I located the laptop, but I couldn't find the keys," Geneva said.

"Are you sure that you looked everywhere in her house? It's very important that those keys are returned," Elizabeth said.

"Yes, I'm sure that I looked everywhere, but I'll look again."

"Yes, do that as soon as possible," Elizabeth said.

Elizabeth said goodbye to Geneva and went back into her house. At the last moment, Geneva decided to keep the keys because it might come in handy to be able to enter any room in International House. And if she did not need them, she would just return the keys to Elizabeth.

\* \* \*

Bradley sat and stared at a wall containing a collage made up of pictures of Victoria. He sat in the small locked room in his basement. This small room was his only refuse from Elizabeth's scolding tongue. He missed the smell of Victoria's body, the softness of her skin and the smoothness of her touch. Even though he had enjoyed such pleasures long before her death, his body still longed to be near and inside her body.

He looked at his watch. It was two o'clock in the afternoon. He pulled out his cell phone and dialed a number.

"I need to see you," Bradley said.

"It will cost you eight thousand."

"What? We have an arrangement," Bradley said.

"Correction, we had an arrangement. Now we have a new arrangement. I will meet you Wednesday afternoon at the usual place. Don't show up if you don't have the money."

The line went dead on the other end and Bradley could only hear the dial tone. He could not find a replacement for Victoria, only a substitute. He did not want to pay more. The goods were not that valuable, but he knew that he would not be able to find someone else so cooperative.

\* \* \*

After Geneva entered Zain's room that evening, Zain turned off the television. Geneva sat on Zain's bed. Zain's room was in the West wing, and she had a direct view of the Nobel House and Victoria's condo from her window on the eighth floor. Crates containing volumes of history books about Jamaica, computer science books and hanging files with photocopies of articles filled every inch of available open space in Zain's room. Zain removed the shelves above her bed and hung photographs of her family members and locations in Montego Bay.

Zain sat in the chair at her desk and adjusted her glasses.

"So the police suspect you of killing your aunt? I can't believe it. But they probably don't have any real evidence against you. Otherwise, they would have arrested you. It sounds like they only have circumstantial evidence and very little of it."

"Circumstantial evidence? You've been watching too much court TV. Detective Peterson said that they did not have any other suspects. Obviously, there are other suspects since I didn't kill her. I just have to find them," Geneva said.

"What do you mean that you have to find them?" Zain asked.

"I mean I'm going to find out who killed my aunt. People go to prison all the time for crimes they didn't commit. I have no intention of being one of them. My aunt had secrets. To be exact, she had ten million secrets. Someone killed her, and I am going to find out who."

"Geneva, the keyword is 'killed'. You're talking about going after a murderer, a cold-blooded killer. You're not a police officer. You're a poet. You should leave the police work to the police. You should get a good lawyer," Zain said.

"I'm going to leave the police work to the police. I'm just going to lead them in the right direction. And the trip begins with Bradley Wilson."

"Bradley Wilson, why him?" Zain asked.

"He cried at the burial. Why would a man cry about the death of his wife's employer? Elizabeth was stone faced the entire time. Also today, I overheard an argument between him and Elizabeth when I returned the laptop. He had an affair with someone," Geneva explained.

"I can count the number of times that I've seen Elizabeth Wilson's facial expression change on one hand. So her behavior at the funeral was not surprising. His office is on campus. We can talk to him tomorrow," Zain said.

"What do you mean by we? I don't want the both of us getting involved in this mess."

Zain smiled. "You're my best friend. I'm already involved. Two minds are always better than one."

Geneva did not try to change Zain's mind. She would help her regardless of Geneva's agreement. And by knowing the extent of Zain's involvement, Geneva could sort of monitor and direct her actions.

"Ok, you can help me. But you do so according to my rules. Got it!" Geneva asked.

"I got it," Zain said.

"To start with I'm going to visit Bradley alone. I don't want it to appear like we are ganging up on him. After all, he may be innocent too."

"I disagree. I think I should go. But if you insist then I won't go," Zaid said.

"I insist indeed," Geneva replied.

# CHAPTER 26

When her mother finally moved into Montgomery Place, Detective Peterson thought about selling her parents' six-bedroom home in the upper middle-class neighborhood of the Jackson Park Highlands. It seemed like the only practical decision especially since she had no immediate plans, and more important, no viable prospects for marriage. But after four years of living in the colonial style house, developing an extensive exercise room and creating a workshop for her miniature housing projects, she knew that she would never sell the house. The house was not just a place to eat, sleep, exercise, and build miniature houses; it was a sanctuary. It was a refuse from a job that never failed to illuminate the cruel nature of her fellow two-legged earthlings.

Like most things, the house reminded her of the good moments in her life such as the joyful presence of her father, the love shared by her parents, her promotion to detective; and it kept the bad moments such as being left at the altar, her father's untimely death, or the first time she fired her gun in the back of her mind. These memories did not make her sad but rather they inspired her to continue forward and to know that she can survive.

Detective Peterson finished her last set on the leg press machine. The exercise room contained the regular weight training and cardio-vascular equipment such as an arm extension, shoulder press, treadmill, and elliptical machine, but to her pride, it also contained two non-traditional items, a rock climbing wall and a Pilates apparatus.

She spent at least sixty minutes a day using the equipment in the room. She did not struggle with the task of exercising like most people because unlike most things in life, completing an exercise routine was one of the few things she could control. She exercised to stay in shape and to obtain the sense of accomplishment that accompanied the completion of an exercise routine.

Her legs were a little wobbly when she got up from the leg press machine. As she headed towards the leg extension machine, the phone rang. She wanted to let the answering machine pick up the call, but she thought that it might be something about the Franklin case, so she changed direction and walked over to the phone and picked it up.

She did not believe who was on the other end of the phone. She asked the man to repeat his name.

"This is Tyler Nelson. My mother and your mother both live at Montgomery Place."

"How did you get my phone number?" She already knew the answer but wanted verbal confirmation.

"Your mother gave me your number. She told me that you would be expecting my call tonight. However, it sounds like you weren't."

"You're correct. I wasn't expecting your call. My mother tends to do things that she really shouldn't like give out my phone number to strangers."

"Well, we're not really strangers per se. I mean I've heard a great deal about you from your mother, and I'm sure she has told you about me. We know each other through third parties but just not first hand. But since we're on the phone now, we might as well make the most of it. What do you think?"

*I think I should change my phone number*, she thought.

"I suppose you make a good point."

"Your mother tells me that you like to make miniature houses. That's fascinating. How long have you been pursuing that hobby?"

"For the past ten years."

"Do you make the little furniture and the little people, too?"

"I make some of the furniture, but most of it I buy already made. I focus my attention on building the structures. I don't have any people occupying the houses."

"I suppose people are really not important for a miniature house.

On the other hand, as you know my job centers around people."

What was his job? She couldn't remember. Every time her mother started talking about him, she would tune her out.

"How did you get started in creating miniature houses?" Tyler continued.

"It's a long story."

"I've got time. Maybe you could tell me the story over a hot cup of green tea? I would suggest coffee but your mother told me that you're really into eating healthy and exercising."

Peterson's patience was gone. She did not like to be interrupted when exercising, and she did not like someone knowing things about her that she did not tell them.

"Hello, are you still there?" Tyler asked.

"Did my mother also tell you that I'm a homicide detective for the Chicago Police Department and right now I'm working on a major murder case? I really have to cut this short."

"No, she didn't. I have the utmost respect for public servants. I didn't mean to bother you. I'd really like to talk to you at a more convenient time. When can we talk again?'

"I really don't know. I'll let you know, but right now I really must go."

She did not wait for a response before she hung up the phone. She wanted to call her mother, but she knew that her mother would simply say that she was only trying to help her unmarried daughter. Her mother thought that the road to happiness was paved with marriage, a house in the suburbs and children.

And in all honesty, Peterson used to feel the same way too until she was left at the altar and men, like deer running from a lion, started to back away from her when they found out about her occupation. Men don't like women who have bigger guns that theirs. This was why her mother did not tell all of those so-called prospective son-in-laws about her daughter's job.

Peterson knew she would have to talk to her mother yet again. And be firm with her. She was not looking forward to the conversation. But if she wanted strange men to stop calling her, she would have to get her mother to stop talking about her and giving out her phone number.

## CHAPTER 27

Margaret had just returned to her room after eating dinner when someone knocked on her door. Before she could walk to the door to open it, the door opened and her Aunt Teresa entered her room. Teresa Kirkwood was her father's only sister. Teresa was a fifty-six-year-old woman who spent every day trying to look twenty-six. She always wore tight pants or short skirts and high-heeled shoes. She went to great expense to make sure her long blonde hair stayed free of grey hair.

"So, you're still alive, I see. I was going to call the police. Why didn't you return my phone calls?" Teresa demanded.

"I didn't want to. What are you doing here?" Margaret asked sharply.

"I'm trying to honor my dear brother's wish and look after his daughter. I was concerned about you especially in light of the murder," Teresa said.

"I'm fine. You can go now," Margaret said, frowning.

"I'll go when I am ready, young lady. What have you been doing with yourself these days? I see you've been making some rather large withdrawals from your account."

"It's my money. I wish you would stop spying on me," Margaret yelled.

"Yes, it is your money. Unfortunately, the court feels that I'm the best person to regulate your spending. And don't raise your voice at me. You should respect your elders."

"You mean you're finally acknowledging that you're old?" Margaret said.

"Remember that the withdrawal limits can be changed at my discretion," Teresa said.

"Why don't you mind your own business and stay out of mine?"

"Why can't you look like a normal thirty-year-old woman? Look at you. Why on earth would anyone with natural blonde hair dye it jet-black, shave off their eyebrows, and wear black every single day. What man is going to want to be with someone who looks likes you? You should at least cut that hair. I'm surprised that you haven't tripped over it yet and hurt yourself," Teresa said.

"Well, I would rather look this than like someone I'm not," Margaret said.

"You're wasting your youth. All of this hocus pocus stuff that you waste money on and visiting your father's grave every week is not healthy," Teresa said.

"Will you leave me alone and get out."

"I told you not to raise your voice at me. I'm only trying to help you," Teresa said.

"Help me by leaving," Margaret said.

"Fine," Teresa said as she walked to the door, opened it and left the room. Margaret locked the door behind her. Every time she had a run-in with her aunt, Margaret reminded herself that everyday Teresa gets older and older, and one day she will die.

## CHAPTER 28

A chill went up Geneva's spine as the cold Thursday morning wind blew through the window in Bradley Wilson's office. Some papers on his desk shifted when he closed the door behind her. He walked behind his desk. "I hope the open window doesn't bother you. It gets rather hot in here to me," Wilson said.

"No, it's fine," Geneva said. It really did bother her. She was already cold. But she was there to get information, so she certainly couldn't start telling the man what to do in his own office.

"What can I do for you today?"

"I wanted to talk to you about my Aunt Victoria," Geneva said.

"Really, I don't know what I can tell you. I barely knew her. Elizabeth knew her the most. Have there been any developments in her case? I have not heard or read anything in the news."

"No, there haven't been any developments. How long did you know my aunt?"

"I only saw her during luncheons or receptions at International House. We only had casual conversations. We usually just said hello to each other. You should really talk to Elizabeth," Wilson said.

"My aunt had a reputation for being a very social person. I always got the impression that everyone knew her, and she knew something personal about everyone."

Bradley stopped rearranging the papers on his desk. "What do you mean by that comment?"

"I mean that she always knew things about people's family life.

You know, she would always ask people about their husbands, wives, children, mothers and et cetera."

"Oh, yes, you're right. She was always asking people about their families."

"You seemed rather upset at the funeral. You cried rather profusely," Geneva said.

"I cried profusely, really? I didn't realize that. I don't do well at funerals. It was sad how your aunt died. You know we hear about these kinds of things on the television, but we are removed from them. But when it hits close to home, it really makes you stop and think about things."

"Do you remember if Elizabeth worked late that night?" Geneva asked.

Bradley picked up some papers from his desk and started leafing through them.

"No, Elizabeth didn't work late that night. We were visiting our daughter, Monica at the U of C Children's hospital."

"I didn't know the two of you had a daughter. Is she ok?"

"Her condition is stable. I really have to get back to work. I'm afraid I can't be more help to you."

"I see, well, thank you for your time. I won't keep you any longer," Geneva said as she stood up.

"You're welcome, anytime," Wilson said.

He sat back down and picked up some papers and started to read them. Geneva walked out of his office. Geneva thought that some truth was missing from Bradley's statements because grown men just don't cry over women unless there's a good reason.

# CHAPTER 29

The sun beamed through the window and awakened the eclectic array of stuffed animals and Winnie the Pooh décor in Monica Wilson's hospital room. With her eyes closed and her hands to her sides, the pale, golden haired little girl laid in the bed with only the beeping sound of a heart monitor and an intravenous drip adding sound to the room. Geneva and Zain walked over to her bedside.

"Should we wake her?" Zain whispered.

"No, I don't think so," Geneva replied softly.

"She's so still. Shouldn't she be moving some," Zain said.

Before Geneva could respond, the door opened and a nurse came into the room. The short, pudgy lady greeted them with a smile full of glowing white teeth.

"Hello, is everything ok?" the nurse asked.

"We think so," Geneva said.

"Why are you whispering?"

"We don't want to wake her," Zain said.

"Well, actually you do want to wake her. She's comatose and has been for the past five years. Since that seems to be news to you, the both of you must not know her."

"No, we don't. We know her parents," Geneva said.

"Her parents said that they visited with her a few weeks ago," Zain said.

"They said that, really? I know that Mr. Wilson has come faithfully every night for the past five years. But no one has seen Mrs.

Wilson since Monica was first admitted," the nurse said.

"So, Mr. Wilson comes every night between eight o'clock and 10 o'clock at night?" Geneva asked.

"Yes, he usually stays past visiting hours."

"So no one has seen Elizabeth Wilson for a while?" Zain asked.

"Yes, that's correct. Why are you two here?"

"We were visiting some one else and thought we would drop by to see their daughter. We didn't know she was comatose," Zain said.

"That's very thoughtful of you. The two of you should stay awhile. And talk to her or you can read to her. That's what her father does when he visits. She usually only has one visitor. So the two of you can be some new voices for her."

Geneva and Zain backed away from the bed as the nurse checked Monica's monitors and wrote something in her chart. Then she tucked her sheets and left the room. Zain walked over to the bookshelf and picked up, *The Three Bears*.

"Maybe we should read the this to her?"

Geneva smiled, "I think she's a little too old for that bedtime story."

Geneva noticed there was a copy of *The Hobbit* next to her bed and that it had a bookmark in it. She sat next to Monica's bed and picked up the book and opened it to the bookmarked page.

"It looks like her father was reading, *The Hobbit* to her. Let's read a chapter to her."

"Ok," Zain said as she pulled up another chair and placed it next to Geneva's.

"What are we going to do now that we know he lied about Elizabeth?" Zain asked.

"I'm going to talk to her about it. But I don't know exactly what I'm going to say."

## CHAPTER 30

Geneva always wanted a sister and soon her fantasy would become a reality. She wanted someone to talk to about men, clothes, and all of those other personal female issues that only women talk about. Geneva often heard other people talk about the difficult relationships that they had with their siblings but these anecdotes never changed her desire to have a sister. She held on to the romantic notion that a sister was a built-in life long friend.

On the phone, Joanna Quinn hesitated to schedule the meeting. This made Geneva wonder if it was Joanna's idea to not have Geneva know about her existence and not her aunt's. Geneva still could not understand why her aunt Victoria hid the truth about her sister for so many years.

Even though most of the tables in the Pancake House on Fifty-first Street were taken, the restaurant did not have its usual long line that Thursday afternoon. Geneva arrived early and was able to get a booth directly across from the entrance. This way she would immediately see Joanna arrive.

In her mind, she rehearsed her first hello. She was glad that she had spent last night writing out her questions and some answers to some anticipated questions from Joanna.

At exactly twelve-thirty, Geneva saw a woman enter the restaurant. The woman walked up to the hostess and then the hostess pointed to the table where Geneva sat. The woman looked at Geneva and smiled. She walked over to the booth and extended her right hand.

"Hello, are you Geneva Anderson?"

Geneva stood up quickly. Her right hip bumped the table so hard that her lemonade spilled. Before Geneva could respond, the woman grabbed the napkins on the table and started to clean up the spill.

"What a mess," Geneva said.

"Oh, don't worry. Accidents happen. Are you Geneva?" the woman repeated.

"Yes, yes, I'm Geneva Anderson." Geneva extended her right hand.

The woman extended her hand again. "It's nice to meet you, I'm Joanna Quinn."

Joanna ended the handshake first. A bus boy came to the table and picked up the wet napkins and wiped off the table with a wet towel. Joanna was a tall woman with light brown skin who wore her hair natural and cut very short. Joanna sat, and Geneva joined her. Geneva looked at Joanna and could not remember a single question from her list. She wanted to pull it out to refer to it but thought that would seem too artificial and anal.

"Well, how are you today?" Joanna asked.

"I'm okay," Geneva said.

Joanna nodded. "Good. This is awkward isn't it?"

"Yes, it's very awkward. I don't know what to say," Geneva said.

Geneva was thinking the same thing, and she was glad that Joanna verbalized that observation.

"I understand. I feel the same way. Why don't I tell you a little bit about myself and then you can do the same in return," Joanna said.

"That sounds like a good plan."

Geneva was glad that she did not have to start. She never knew where to start when she had to tell people about herself. She liked it when people simply asked her direct questions. Joanna took off her scarf and coat.

"Well, let's see. I was born and raised in Chicago. I'm a widow and childless. I'm fifty-five years old and in between jobs at the moment. I attended Chicago State University. I didn't know what I wanted to do. But I needed a job. So after graduating, I worked as a secretary at the University of Chicago. I kept that job for over twenty years. I don't watch any television. I don't even own a television. I read the newspapers and magazines. I really can't stand television. I think it makes people intellectually weak minded," Joanna said.

Geneva hung on her every word. They had several things in common except for their television viewing habits. Geneva didn't watch much television, but she did like the television that she watched. Geneva's cheek started to twitch, and she swallowed hard. It was her turn to talk.

"Okay, well, let's see. I'm not a very good cook. It's hit or miss. I watch television but mostly news and informational programming. I'm single. I've never been married, and I don't have any children. And I don't work because I have a writing fellowship. I'm working on my first book of poetry, and I attend a weekly poetry writing workshop." Geneva felt like she was babbling.

Joanna smiled and nodded as Geneva spoke. Joanna's demeanor was that of a woman who had seen her share of bad days and worst nights. The whiteness of her teeth when she smiled offset the dark circles under eyes. Joanna had a past that Geneva wanted to know about.

"Do you like to read poetry?" Geneva asked.

"Yes, I do. I must confess that I have not read much of it, but I do enjoy it. I would like to read some of your poetry if you wouldn't mind."

"No, I wouldn't mind at all. I hope you like it," Geneva said.

"I'm sure that I would enjoy it very much," Joanna said.

Geneva wanted to ask her about who raised her, but she was not sure how to go about it. Joanna finished her drink.

"What was our mother like?" Joanna asked.

Joanna opened the door. Geneva took a deep breath to find the words.

"I really can't answer that question very well. I think she was very nice and that she loved me. I'm sure that she loved the both of us. I'm not sure what happened with you, but when I was a baby, my father beat our mother very badly one day, and she was left severely brain damaged. All I can remember is her being a shell of a human being before she died. I know very little about her. I grew up in an orphanage. Victoria was only ten years older than me. So she could not raise me. But when I turned eighteen, she really started helping me by providing for my education."

Joanna continued to nod, but she did not have any other expression on her face. Geneva wondered if she had any sympathy for their mother.

"My understanding is that our mother could not take care of me, and as a result, the state took me away from her. I was put in a foster home when I was three years old. It was a good home. I stayed with the same family for fifteen years. I had to leave when I turned eighteen. I suppose she did the best she could under the circumstances. This world is hard on women, children and the elderly," Joanna said.

*She didn't hate our mother*, Geneva thought. Geneva was glad that Joanna did not have any bitter feelings about what had happened. Joanna certainly may have been angry about her childhood when she was younger, but now she seemed to be at peace with it. At least she was not saying or implying that she hated their mother.

"I'm glad that you were in a good foster home," Geneva said.

"Even though I was in a foster home, your childhood was much worse than mine. How did you manage to survive it?" Joanna asked.

"Escapism. I escaped using books and television. The people in the books and on television had better lives than mine. So I focused on their problems and lives and not my own," Geneva said.

"I suppose I practice escapism, too. I read a lot as well. The couple that I lived with took in several children at one time. When I lived with them, they had nine other foster children all of whom came from different ethnic backgrounds. We lived in one of those big mansions in Evanston. So my surroundings growing up were rather peaceful and pleasant," Joanna said.

"That's wonderful that you had a good childhood despite a rocky start. Did you know about me before Victoria's death?" Geneva asked.

"No, I found out about you when Mr. Nicholson called me. I didn't even know Victoria," Joanna said.

Geneva and Joanna spent the remainder of the afternoon talking about clothes, men and poetry. Geneva liked Joanna, and it seemed like Joanna's feelings were mutual. They didn't laugh much. Joanna was not the giggly type. But she was very attentive. Geneva wanted to see more of her. But, Joanna was unable to set another meeting date. Geneva tried to not read too much into her hesitancy, but unfortunately, it was her nature to do just that.

## CHAPTER 31

After Deepa arrived, Bradley closed the curtains to the hotel room at the Ramada Inn. She was twenty minutes late. He expected to see her when he arrived since she's the one who told him not to bother showing up if he wasn't going to pay the new price. She stood in front of the dresser with her back to him, looked in the mirror and combed her long black hair with her fingertips. He sat on the bed and took off his shoes. He started to take of his shirt when she turned around.

"Where's the money?" Deepa demanded.

"It's on the table next to the television," Bradley said.

Deepa looked at the table where the television was sitting and walked over to it. She picked up the envelope and started counting the money.

"It's all there. Don't you trust me?" Bradley said smiling.

"No! After all, look where you are?" Deepa said.

After she counted the money, she put it in her purse. Bradley turned back the covers on the bed, fluffed the pillows and placed them in the center of the bed.

"Do you talk to Geneva Anderson much?" Bradley asked.

"No, why would I?" Deepa said sharply.

Bradley was not surprised by her response. Deepa did not talk to people she considered beneath her. And Deepa considered most people to be in that category. He liked this aspect of her personality because it meant that their involvement would not get complicated. With Deepa, it would always be about the money and nothing else.

"She visited me yesterday. She wanted to know about my relationship with her aunt. I thought maybe the two of you talked since you both lived in the same place," Bradley said.

"No, we don't talk. But I'm not surprised that she asked you about Victoria since you were crying like a baby at her funeral. What were you thinking? Didn't you think someone would notice a grown man crying over his wife's boss?"

Bradley was only concerned about the answer to his question and not Deepa's critique of his behavior. So he continued with his objective for the afternoon. He reached down beside the bed and picked up a bag. He reached inside the bag and took out five black satin scarves, a bottle of chocolate syrup, a bottle of caramel syrup, and a can of whipped cream and sat them on the nightstand next to the bed.

"Do you think she knows about your affair with Victoria?" Deepa asked.

"No, she knows nothing," Bradley said.

"If she doesn't know now, you need to make sure that she doesn't find out later. You don't want Elizabeth to find out about Victoria or us. Maybe you should search Victoria's condo to make sure Victoria didn't leave anything behind connecting the two of you," Deepa said.

"Do I look like a cat burglar to you? And it's not necessary; Victoria was not the sentimental type. There wouldn't be anything in her house about me and her," Bradley said.

He was pretty sure that there wasn't anything in Victoria's house about their affair, but he wasn't so sure about his embezzlement from the university's endowment. Even though she was dead, the tape that she made with his bedroom confession may still be alive and well. Deepa was right. He had to search Victoria's condo and the sooner, the better.

"Well, you can never be too careful," Deepa said.

"You're right, you can't be. Take off your clothes," Bradley said.

Deepa slipped out of her shoes and dress. He liked it when she remembered not to wear under garments and stockings. She lay in the center of the bed with her head on the pillows. He picked up one of the black satin scarves, wrapped it around her left wrist and tied the scarf to the headboard. He repeated the process with her right arm. He was starting to perspire already. His armpits were moist, and he felt a little perspiration on his forehead. He picked up a third scarf, wrapped it around her left knee, lifted up her leg and tied the scarf to the headboard. He repeated the same bondage method with Deepa's right leg.

This left her lying in the center of the bed with her arms tied at the wrists, her legs spread eagle, bent at the knee and tied to the headboard. He pulled on each of the scarves to make sure that they were secure. Then, he picked up the fifth scarf and wrapped it around her eyes. Afterwards, he took off his pants, placed the whipped cream and the bottles of syrup at the foot of the bed. He climbed back onto the bed and sat on his knees between her legs. After he shook up the whipped cream, he sprayed it from her left knee, across her pubic area, and to her right knee. He continued to spray the whipped cream in this fashion until the can was empty. The more he sprayed the more erect he became. He picked up the chocolate syrup and squeezed it over the carpet of whipped cream that he had just created. The chocolate syrup was followed by caramel syrup.

Deepa laid perfectly still just the way he liked her. He inhaled a deep breath and exhaled it. He bent over and started to enjoy the sweet mixture that he had just created. As his mouth made its way from her left knee to her right knee, the goose bumps started to grow on his body one-by-one. These moments with Deepa were not about sex. They never had intercourse.

After Victoria, sex was meaningless to him. He only wanted to make love, and he wanted to make love to Victoria. But Victoria was gone, and his wife was not an option. He would never pay for sex, but no price was too great for submission, thus, he was able to tolerate Deepa's infernal mouth.

# CHAPTER 32

The underground fencing club, The Mouliner, was in the sub-basement of a gentlemen's club. The two places had more in common than one might think. Both provided unconventional entertainment to a restricted audience in a place that did not allow daylight to penetrate its interior. The unregulated fencing bouts at The Mouliner were conducted inside of a boxing ring surrounded by football type seating stands.

Just above the boxing ring, on the main level, young women with thin legs and flexible bodies danced on and around mirrored polls on a stage surrounded by the eyes and twenty dollar bills of eager men.

Only club members could enter the gentlemen's club and visitors had to be invited by a club member. Likewise, only people invited by the fencers could watch and bet on the bouts at The Mouliner. Xavier refused to take Zain to see Heather fight so she got one of the fighters who used to fence with the university club to take her inside.

Zain watched Heather complete her last bout by aggressively engaging her opponent's blade, pushing her opponent back and then executing a jumping lunge accompanied by a forward thrust. The audience erupted into applause as a severed hand fell to the floor. The cheers vibrated off the walls when Heather raised both of her arms and her opponent fell to his knees clutching his handless arm.

When Heather left the fighting area and headed back to the locker room, Zain followed her. Heather turned a corner and just as Zain started to turn the same corner, a hand grabbed her left arm. She turned around and came face-to-face with Xavier.

"You don't belong here. You need to go," Xavier said.

"You're wrong. I need to be here," Zain replied.

The locker room door opened and closed behind them and a few seconds later, Heather was standing with Xavier and Zain.

"I knew you couldn't get enough of me Xavier," Heather said.

"Think again. I've had enough of you."

"Have you had enough of being a coward?"

"Shut up"

"You were good. You could've been great if you hadn't lost your nerve."

"Shut up, please," Xavier yelled.

A man approached the three of them. "Hello, everyone. What's all the shouting about?"

"Nothing," Xavier said.

"I see that it's nothing. It's a very loud nothing," the man said.

The man extended his hand towards Zain. "Since these two won't introduce me, I'll introduce myself. I'm Paul Jones."

"Hello, I'm Zain Valdez."

"It's nice to meet you. Did you enjoy the show?" Paul asked.

"It was interesting," Zain replied.

"It wasn't interesting. It was horrific. We need to go, now," Xavier said as he took Zain's arm and pulled her down the hall towards the exit.

Xavier and Zain drove back to I-House in silence. The snow started to fall faster when Xavier pulled up in front of I-House. He took the key out of the ignition and turned off the headlights.

"Let's go," he said. He unfastened his seat belt and opened the car door when Zain placed her hand on his shoulder.

"No wait, can we talk for a minute?"

Xavier turned and looked at her and then closed the car door.

"What do you want to talk about?"

"What was Heather talking about when she said that you lost your nerve?"

Xavier placed his hands on the steering wheel and stared straight ahead.

"I used to fence at The Mouliner. I was bored with the conventional fencing at the university. So I started at The Mouliner. I won one hundred bouts in a row, and I made over one hundred thousand dollars. One night I was fencing a freshman. I should have stopped, but he was cocky. And I was too arrogant to ignore him. He tried a trick maneuver and failed to execute it properly and ended up on top of my sword. He died instantly. It was ruled an accident. Afterwards, I stopped fencing, and I sold my equipment."

"I'm sorry that happened to you. But it wasn't your fault. He knew what he was doing. He knew the risk."

"Yes, he knew but so did I. I could've lightened up, backed off or simply never have started in the first place. Fencing at The Mouliner is dangerous. You saw what happened tonight. He got off easy. Do you want to lose a limb or your life over something that happened in high school?"

"No, I don't. But I also want to prove to myself that I can stand up to Heather. Will you help me to fence against her?"

"No, I won't help you to kill yourself."

"Are my chances better or worst with your help?"

"They would be better."

"Well then, when do we begin?"

"Tomorrow morning."

\* \* \*

Heather sat behind her desk while Paul stood in front of her. He reached into his inside coat pocket and pulled out a white letter size envelope. He threw the envelope on the desk. She picked it up and counted the contents.

"What is this?" she demanded.

"It's your cut from the bets," Paul said.

"There should be more here. This place has been packed all week. I want my share," she yelled as she stood up and walked from behind her desk and stood directly in front of Paul.

"Don't raise your voice to me. People think you're in charge but we know the truth. You'll do what I say, when I say it. May I remind you that the bets are illegal? No one knows about me but everyone knows about you."

"Maybe we should end our partnership."

Paul grabbed Heather's neck with his right hand, and placed his left hand on her torso and pushed her up against the wall.

"Look, blondie, no one ends anything with me. We are together until I say it is over. Got it."

Heather did not reply.

"I can't hear you," Paul said as he pulled her away from the wall and pushed her back against it again.

"Got it," Heather whispered.

# CHAPTER 33

After eating dinner, Geneva decided to spend Friday evening doing her laundry and told herself that she would actually fold the clothes this time and not just leave them in the bag. She really was getting tired of living out of laundry bags after she washed her clothes. It was a bad habit, but she hated folding clothes.

As usual, she had two bags of laundry to wash. Every time she promised herself that she was going to do her laundry every week, but it was always every two weeks instead. Geneva picked up one of the bags and opened the door to go downstairs. When she opened the door, Deepa was standing in front of Geneva's door.

"Hi, I was just about to knock. Are you busy?" Deepa asked.

"I was just about to do my laundry," Geneva replied.

"May I come in?"

Annoyed, Geneva dropped the bag. "Wait a minute."

Geneva could not hold the bag and let Deepa into her room at the same time. Geneva closed the door and placed the laundry bag in her closet and then reopened the door and let Deepa into her room.

"What do you want to talk about, Deepa?"

Deepa pulled out the desk chair and sat. She crossed her legs and proceeded to casually gaze around the room while simultaneously fixing her hair with her fingers.

"I just wanted to see how you were doing and to find out if there was any news about your aunt's case," Deepa said.

"I'm okay. There haven't been any developments so far."

Geneva did not know why Deepa would care about how she was doing. She certainly was not going to admit that she was a suspect in the case. Geneva didn't even tell Joanna about the police's suspicions.

Deepa smoothed her skirt and adjusted herself in the chair as if posing for an invisible photographer.

"I see. I've not heard anything in the news lately. You know these things become history so fast. Do they have any suspects?"

"I don't know about any suspects. I'm sure that the police are doing the best that they can. Did you know my aunt well?"

"Some of the other residents were asking me about the case to see if I knew anything. People always come to me for information about various things."

Geneva wanted to laugh out loud. But she held it in and simply cleared her throat.

"Really, some residents were asking you questions? I see," Geneva said.

Before she could respond further, someone knocked on her door. She hoped that it was Zain so she could create an excuse to get rid of Deepa. She opened the door, and it was Su.

"Ladies, what's going on?" Su asked.

"Not, much," Geneva said.

"What are you two talking about?" Su asked.

"Deepa says that some residents were asking her questions about my aunt's case."

"I don't think it is some. Everyone I see has been talking about it. It's scary knowing that someone was killed in the same building where you live," Su said.

"Deepa, I think you can just tell them that the case is progressing along," Geneva said.

"I see," Deepa said.

"Where's Zain?' Su asked.

"I don't really know, why?" Geneva replied.

"Tonight is ladies night at the casino. Why don't the four of us go?"

Deepa stood up and adjusted her skirt again. "I really must decline. But the three of you should go. I'm sure that the three of you would fit right in." She looked at her watch and continued. "I really have to get back to the hospital," Deepa continued as she walked to the door and opened it.

"Thanks for stopping by," Geneva said.

Geneva grabbed the door and held it. Deepa left the room and never turned around again as she walked down the hallway. Geneva wondered what educated person would turn to Deepa for information about anything more than when the next sale at Nordstrom's was being held. Geneva never understood what Xavier saw in her besides looks. But as she well knew, looks are all that mattered to most men. Deepa was one of those fortunate creatures on the planet that commanded the attention of men. Geneva tried to adhere to the adage that one should hate the game and not the player. But Deepa did not make that easy to do.

"I'm glad that she said no. What did she mean by 'the three of us will fit in'?" Su asked.

"Who knows and who cares? But, I'm afraid I can't go either. I'm not much of a gambler."

"You don't have to gamble. You can just watch me work the tables. We can drink, eat, and check out the guys."

"No, smoky casinos just don't excite me."

"The smoking is not that bad. You need to relax. You've always been wrapped tight. Now you're like a balloon with way too much air. All you need is a needle to pop you. I just think it would be less painful, if you let the air out slowly instead of all at once."

Geneva cleared her throat and took a deep breath. She knew that Su was right. She was wrapped tight. She needed to let go. But she wasn't sure that a casino was the best place for that event to take place.

"I appreciate your concern. But I don't think I'm going to explode today."

"Will you at least think about going?"

"Yes, I'll think about it. Now, I really need to do my laundry otherwise I'm going to be walking around without any underwear."

"What's wrong with that? It's one way to save money."

"And another way is to not go to the casino," Geneva said as she picked up her laundry bag again and the two of them left her room.

## CHAPTER 34

The most stressful part of building a miniature house was by far the construction of the exterior and interior walls. And this time, it was no different. Peterson spent her Saturday morning carefully arranging the small pieces of wood and double and triple checking to make sure that she had not left out a piece. After she confirmed the arrangement of the wall pieces, she glued them together.

When the glue dried, she started one of the easiest tasks for a miniaturist; she began to wallpaper the interior walls. A few seconds later the phone rang, and she hoped that it was not Tyler Nelson calling back.

"Did you trace the call?" Peterson asked.

"Yes, it came from a pay phone? I want you to get over there right away and arrest her," Captain Ingram said.

"You mean after I search her room."

"I meant I want you to arrest her whether you find the murder weapon or not."

"Don't you think it's a little too convenient for us to find the murder weapon in her room? Why would she keep it so close?"

"Who knows and who cares? She has it and that's all that matters."

"Well, I have to get the warrant."

"Done! I have it with me. I'll meet you there with it."

The phone went dead and Peterson could only hear the dial tone.

\* \* \*

Detective Peterson commenced the search of Geneva's room while Captain Ingram stood in the doorway and a uniformed officer stood in the hallway. Peterson did not want the uniformed officer to help her and knew that Ingram would not help. He just wanted to be present when Geneva was arrested.

It did not take her long to search the three dresser drawers and one closet. She pulled the bed away from the wall and found nothing. She intentionally saved the bookshelves for last because she would have to pull every book off the shelf. When she turned to face the bookshelves, and scanned the items on them, she noticed on the second shelf, a shiny gold tip peeping out from the top of an oversized book. She reached up, picked up the book, and opened it to where the object was located. A pointed letter opener with dried blood on it was inside of the book.

"That's it. Let's find her," Ingram said.

"I think we should take her down to the station for questioning but not formally arrest her until forensics confirms that this is the murder weapon with Franklin's blood."

"You can think all you want Peterson. But I want you to arrest Geneva Anderson today and now."

\* \* \*

Geneva was staring out of the window when someone knocked on the library door. And then the door opened. Detective Peterson and another man entered the library.

"Geneva Anderson, stand up," Detective Peterson said.

Geneva stood. "You are under arrest for the murder of Victoria Franklin. Please, turn around and place your hands behind your back," Detective Peterson said.

Geneva did not move. Detective Peterson took hold of Geneva's right arm and turned her around.

"You have the right to remain silent. If you do not remain silent, anything you say can and will be used against you in a court of law.

You have the right to an attorney. If you cannot afford an attorney, one will be appointed for you," the man said.

"You're making a mistake. I didn't kill my aunt."

"The evidence says otherwise," the man said.

"What evidence? What are you talking about?"

"I think it's best for us to answer those questions down at the station," Detective Peterson said.

Tears streamed down her face as Detective Peterson led her out of the library.

# CHAPTER 35

Geneva was taken to the Cook County Jail at Twenty-sixth and California for booking. It took four hours to complete the booking process. She was stripped searched, fingerprinted, and photographed. When she arrived at the jail, she made her one phone call to Zain and asked her to see if Henry Nicholson was back in town, and if so, to ask him to represent her. Zain said that she would contact Nicholson and visit her afterwards.

It was early afternoon when Geneva was told that she had a visitor. One female sheriffs' deputy accompanied Geneva into the visitor room. Geneva was swimming in her orange jumpsuit. The bright fluorescent light made it easy to see the many fingerprints on the thick bulletproof glass that separated inmates from visitors. The walls were off-white with cracked plaster and various scratches and dents throughout them. Geneva could not imagine how many parents, wives, siblings, and children that glass had separated.

Zain was sitting in the room when Geneva entered. She smiled as Geneva approached the seating area. Geneva sat as Zain picked up the receiver. Geneva followed suit and picked up the receiver on her end.

"Are you okay?" Zain asked.

"Yes, I'm okay. Did you call Nicholson?"

"Yes, he said he would come by later this afternoon. He said that you will probably have to spend the night in jail. He thought he could post your bail tomorrow."

"Thank you for calling him. Does anyone else know that I have been arrested?"

"Not that I know of," Zain said.

"Can you call Dr. Zimmerman and let him know?"

"Yes, I'll call him. Is there anything else that you want me to do?"

"No, not now," Geneva replied.

The deputy came up behind Geneva. "Time's up."

Geneva hung up the receiver and the deputy took Geneva's left arm and escorted her out of the room.

* * *

After she saw Zain, Geneva was escorted to the same interview room where she was first accused of murdering her aunt. The same sticky spot was still on the table. In anticipation of its forthcoming pain, her butt started to ache before she even sat down. Questions raced through her mind. What made the police arrest her, why haven't they told her, how long would it take for her mug shot to be on the local news, would the judge grant bail?

She did not know if she could survive jail much less prison. Confined spaces never bothered her before but that was probably because she had only been an elevator. She wondered if the word future applied to her anymore. A prison sentence means no marriage, childbearing years lost, and career destroyed. Her prison sentence would not end when she walked out of the prison, it would continue until the day she died, assuming she lived to walk out of prison. She continued to sit in that room and thought about these things and the fact that she may not have a future.

# CHAPTER 36

When Detective Peterson put the phone down, she saw Captain Ingram's reflection in her computer monitor as he stood behind her. She spun around in her chair to face him.

"The lab results are back and the blood on the letter opener is Victoria Franklin's," Ingram said.

"How do you know that?" Peterson asked.

"I told the lab to call me first when the results came in."

"I see. Are you taking over this case?"

"I'm managing this case. I want you to lean on Anderson to get a confession. She's in interview room two."

"There were no fingerprints on the letter opener. I think she's being framed."

"I think she's a murderer. There's no proof that she's being framed. On the other hand, we have proof that points to her guilt. She had motive, the inheritance; she had opportunity, no alibi; and she had the murder weapon in her room, hid out."

"But, the murder weapon didn't even have Franklin's prints on it. Why would she bother to wear gloves, use it to kill with and then leave it stained with blood in her room? The anonymous caller could be involved."

"Maybe the caller is involved or maybe it's a friend of hers who decided to be a good citizen,"

"What about the letter opener?"

"What about it? Criminals are not smart people. That's why we have jobs. Now, am I in room two or are you?"

Detective Peterson picked up the Franklin case file as she got up from her chair and walked out of the squad room and towards interview room two.

* * *

Detective Peterson blinked her eyes when she entered the interview room and sat directly across from Geneva. She leaned back in her chair with her arms crossed in front of her chest and stared into Geneva's eyes. Geneva wanted to say something but decided that it would be wiser to stay silent.

"We got a call this morning from someone who said that we would find the murder weapon that killed your aunt in your room. We searched your room and found a blood stained letter opener. The lab just confirmed that the blood belonged to your aunt."

Peterson uncrossed her arms and placed her arms on the table and interlaced her hands.

"It's your turn to talk. Did you murder your aunt?"

"No, I did not."

"How do you explain the phone call and the letter opener?"

"Isn't it obvious that the person who made the call set me up?"

"Is it obvious or just possible?"

"I did not kill my aunt."

"You've told me that already. Do you know a man named Devon Bannister?"

"No, who is he?"

"He ..." Before Detective Peterson could finish her sentence, the door opened and a man entered the room.

"This is Captain Larry Ingram in case you were wondering," Peterson said.

"Will you give us a moment, Detective Peterson," Ingram said. He held the door for Peterson to leave. She stared at him for a second and then stood up and walked to the doorway. But before she crossed the threshold of the door, Henry Nicholson approached the doorway.

"I'm Henry Nicholson and I represent Ms. Anderson. I would like to speak with my client alone."

As Nicholson stepped forward, Peterson moved to the side and he entered the room.

"We have overwhelming evidence against your client. It would be wise for her to cooperate," Ingram said.

"It would behoove you to let a court of law make that determination," Nicholson said as he placed his briefcase on the table and sat across from Geneva.

"Excuse us."

Ingram let the door swing as he stepped out of the room. Peterson caught the door and closed it behind her as she left the room too.

* * *

"Thank you for agreeing to represent me," Geneva said.

"No problem," Nicholson replied. "Unfortunately, I cannot get you out on bail until tomorrow morning. This means that you will have to spend the night in jail," Nicholson said.

"I understand," Geneva said.

"I know about the letter opener," Nicholson said. "Do you have any idea how it got into your room?"

"No, I don't. But obviously, it was planted, maybe by the anonymous caller. Why would I keep the murder weapon?"

"Logical, but unfortunately, people are known to keep all sorts of souvenirs after a crime. I have to be honest with you. It doesn't look good for you. Your aunt is murdered, you find the body, you don't have an alibi, you're her sole heir and the murder weapon was found in your room. The anonymous caller may know something, but right now all fingers are pointing to you. Don't talk to anyone about this case, and don't talk to the police."

"I won't talk to the police," Geneva said.

Geneva knew that all roads led to her. She had to get herself out of this mess, one way or another.

# CHAPTER 37

After the cell door closed behind her, Geneva turned around and stood within the two feet of floor space that sat between the two sets of bunk beds.

"Come on in and get comfy," said a woman, whose long blond hair was brighter than her skin. "I'm Randy, what's your name?" she continued.

"Geneva."

"Well, Geneva there's no neutrality here. But, it's your lucky day, usually the last in gets the top bunk, but Francis here decided to hang top. Go on take the bottom bunk."

Geneva walked over to the bunk bed and sat on the bottom bed. The thin woman that Randy referred to as Francis was laying on her side on the top bunk above Randy. She had short, brunette hair and her glowing blue eyes were staring into space.

"So you're the one they got for the Franklin murder?"

"How do you know that?"

"Word spreads fast in this place. Don't worry. There are people here who have done a lot worst than you."

"I didn't kill my aunt. I'm being framed."

"You learn quickly. That's good. Too bad Francis here can't use that defense. After lettin' her hubby beat her for fifteen years in their posh Barrington home, she decided to walk into his office yesterday and shoot him to death. She should've waited until the bastard got home and then took him out."

Geneva agreed, but she did not respond.

"Why are you here?" Geneva asked.

"Well, ya see, I'm just a workin' girl tryin' to make a livin'. A cop got me. Occasionally, the city tries to crack down on the bad elements. So the vice squad sets up stings. It wasn't a lucky day for me."

"I see."

Because of her long red nails, dyed blond hair, and thick eyelashes, Geneva thought that she might be a hooker.

"Don't say nothin' to the cops, no matter what they tell you. Get a high priced lawyer."

"I have an excellent attorney."

"You have a chance," Francis said.

"What? She speaks finally. I've been in here with her for over five hours, and she ain't said a word," Randy said.

"I wouldn't have stood a chance even if I had killed him at home. They always convict women who kill their abusive husbands. I should've killed him fifteen years ago when he started hitting me. I would probably be getting out of prison now."

"Woulda, coulda, shoulda, no sense in cryin' over spilled milk. You might be goin' to prison but at least he got his. And you'll probably go to one of those nice federal prisons because he was a federal judge," Randy said.

"I suppose you'll be getting out tomorrow," Francis said.

"You bet; I'm outta here. What about you Geneva?" Randy asked.

"I'll be posting bail tomorrow."

"That's good. I don't think they're goin' to let little Francis here out on bail. Bein' out on bail will allow you to pursue other options too if you don't think your case will go well," Randy said.

"How many times have you been arrested?" Geneva asked.

"I really don't remember. It doesn't matter in my line of work. I used to be a stripper, but I gained weight and couldn't get work. I thought about goin' to Vegas, but there's a ton of competition out there. Go ahead ask me, you know you want to," Randy said.

"How do you know?"

"Everyone always wants to know."

"What's it like to be with so many men?" Geneva asked.

"It's nothin'. It's a business transaction. Most of my guys are ok. I've only had a few rough ones. But unlike Francis, at least I knew what I was gettin' into. In this business, there are risks. So what do you do?"

"I'm a poet. I'm working on my first book. I used to be a web site designer."

"Ah, you're one of those creative types, nice," Randy said.

The lights went out in the cell but only dimmed in the hall.

"It's bedtime ladies. Good night and don't let the bedbugs bite," Randy said.

"Geneva, can you recite one of your poems for us?" Francis asked.

"Are you sure that you want to hear poetry," Geneva asked.

"Yes, I probably won't hear any again for a while," Francis said.

"Ok, give me a few minutes."

Geneva racked her brain trying to recall a cheerful or uplifting poem for Francis. But she quickly realized that most of her poetry was not very cheerful or uplifting. This realization begged the question is her poetry really doing anything for her readers or is it all self serving.

"I'm afraid I don't really have a lot of uplifting poetry in my collection. At least, I can't seem to recall one at the moment."

"Don't worry about it bein' up liftin'. I don't think Superman could lift up Francis at this point. Just recite somethin' for us," Randy said.

"Ok, then, this is called, *Truth Has a Secret*."

"Truth can hurt when it comes from a friend.
Truth can kill when it is distorted.
Truth can destroy when it is hidden.
Truth can burden you when asked to hold a secret.
Truth can imprison you when the lies flow.
Can we, should we always tell the truth?"

"That was nice, thank you," Francis said.

"And it's true too which makes it even better," Randy said.

Geneva laid flat on her back. She was tired, but she did not want to sleep because she did not want to wake up in a cell tomorrow or any day. She reasoned that if she never went to sleep, then she never had to worry about waking up.

## CHAPTER 38

While Zain sat at her laptop reading her e-mail, she wondered how Geneva was doing. She started to pick up the phone to call Mr. Nicholson when she heard a knock at her door. She opened the door and Elizabeth Wilson was there.

"I heard about Geneva's arrest, and I wanted to know how she was doing," Elizabeth asked.

"I visited her briefly. She said she was ok," Zain responded.

"Will she be getting out on bail?"

"Yes, I think so. I think she'll get out tomorrow."

"Good, I'm glad to hear that. Do you know why they arrested her?" Elizabeth asked.

"No, I don't know any of the details," Zain responded.

"When she comes home, tell her that I asked about her."

"I will."

As Elizabeth turned and placed her hand on the doorknob, someone knocked on the door. Zain stepped in front of Elizabeth and opened the door. It was Deepa. Zain let her into the room.

"Zain, is it true that Geneva murdered her aunt?"

"No, that's not true," Elizabeth said.

"But the police arrested her. They would only do that if she were guilty," Deepa said.

"People are arrested all the time but it doesn't mean that they're guilty. That's why this country has a court system," Zain said.

"Zain's right. Geneva has only been arrested. She still has to stand trial," Elizabeth said.

"Why did they arrest her?" Deepa asked.

"We don't know," Elizabeth replied.

"Well, it's just unbelievable that she was even arrested. I didn't even know that Geneva and her aunt didn't get along," Deepa said.

"Why are you saying that they didn't get along?" Zain asked.

"Well, I mean if she was arrested, the police must of found some information indicating some sort of discord between the two."

"They got along find as far as I know," Zain said.

"Yes, that's correct as far as you know. But there is a lot that you don't know," Deepa said.

"It's getting late, and I have to get up early," Zain said.

"Yes, Deepa and I should go," Elizabeth said as she stepped past Deepa and opened the door.

As Elizabeth and Deepa left her room, Zain began to share Geneva's loathing for Deepa. Deepa was so concerned about the arrest that she didn't even bother to ask about how Geneva was doing. Zain thought about calling Nicholson, but it was now too late. She would wait until the morning.

* * *

The Sunday morning sunshine beamed through Margaret's window as she sat up in bed. She wondered how Geneva's first night in jail went. The local news stations reported the arrest. Margaret also learned about Geneva's arrest because the front desk clerk saw the police take her out of the building in handcuffs. Because the sun started to bother her eyes, she got up to close the drapes in her room, but the phone rang before she got to the window. She looked at the caller ID. It was Elizabeth Wilson. And as usual, she let it ring five more times.

"What on earth is going on?" Elizabeth demanded.

"What are you talking about?" Margaret asked.

"Geneva was arrested yesterday."

"And what does that have to do with me?" Margaret asked.

"That's what I would like to know. Did you have anything to do with her arrest?" Elizabeth asked.

"I would not worry about Geneva. She will get out on bail."

"This is getting out of control. Geneva should not have been arrested, and you know it," Elizabeth said.

"I know that if the police arrested her then they must have had a good reason do so," Margaret said. "Now stop whining. And don't bother me unless you have something important to say." Margaret then hung up the phone.

* * *

Detective Peterson drove down Jeffrey Boulevard on her way to church with her mother.

"Is it true that that young woman killed her aunt?"

"I can't discuss the case, Mom."

"I know. But it's such a shame."

Peterson agreed with her mother even though she could not express it verbally. It was a shame because there was no way to prove a link between Deepa and Devon, no way to disprove Bradley's alibi because the security cameras at the children's hospital showed him arriving and leaving and none of the hospitals were missing the drugs norcuron or hexachorophane. It was a shame indeed.

Peterson turned right onto Eighty-seventh Street.

"Are you going to call Tyler back?"

"Mom, how can you ask me that. Why on earth did you give that man my phone number?"

"Because I knew that you would never call him, if I gave you his number."

"I want you to please stop trying to set me up with the sons, grandsons and nephews of your neighbors and church members. It's embarrassing. I'll get married, when I get married."

"You're not going to get married if you don't date. I just don't want you to be alone when you're my age. I have you, but who will you have?"

Peterson parked the car across the street from the church.

"We should go in," Peterson said.

"You don't know, do you?" Mrs. Peterson asked.

"No, mom, I don't know."

## CHAPTER 39

On Sunday morning, Geneva pleaded not guilty at her arraignment and was let out on a one million dollar bail. She arrived back at International House later that afternoon. Before she went to her room, she went to the basement storage room and retrieved a black duffle bag. When she reached her room, Zain greeted her.

"You didn't have to wait here for me," Geneva said.

"I know. Are you ok?" Zain asked.

"I suppose. I'm just tired, and I need a shower."

"I understand. What's in the bag?"

"Oh, nothing. Just some more sweaters."

Geneva opened her door, and Zain followed her inside.

"Last night Elizabeth and Deepa came by to see me and they asked about you."

"They came together?"

"No, separately. Elizabeth was first and then Deepa. Elizabeth really seemed to be concerned about you. I was surprised. She seemed to be sincere."

"That's good to hear. It will make talking to her easier. What did Deepa want?"

"I'm not really sure. I don't think she wanted anything. She was just being her noisy self."

"Listen, I really need to take a shower. Can you call and order some food for us and meet the delivery guy?"

"Sure, no problem."

When Zain left, Geneva picked up her phone.

"Yes, Mr. Madison. Is your 1995 Saturn still available for sale?"

"Yes, it is," Madison said.

"I would like to buy it and pick it up tomorrow morning. I'll pay you in cash."

"No, problem."

Geneva hung up the phone and immediately dialed another number.

"Do you have any garage spaces for rent?" Geneva asked.

"Yes, we do," the man said.

"I would like to rent one for a 1995 Saturn. Can I bring the car there tomorrow morning?"

"Yes, anytime up until six o'clock."

After she hung up the phone, she undressed and took a shower. She felt like something was crawling on her skin. She stayed in the shower for an hour. Geneva wanted the soap and water to wash away the stench of the jail and her murder charge.

After getting dressed, Geneva sat in her desk chair and stared at the duffle bag on her bed. She knew innocent people went to prison everyday for crimes they did not commit. If she did not find her aunt's killer, she needed a Plan B. The black duffle bag was her Plan B. After spending one night in jail, it became very clear to Geneva that rather than go to prison for a crime that she did not commit, she would rather spend her life in hiding.

Geneva stood and opened the duffle bag. So far the bag contained a hundred thousand in cash, clothes and various maps of Mexico, Canada, and the back roads of the United States. Geneva started to add items to this bag the day Detective Peterson told her that she was a suspect in the case. The court seized her passport at the arraignment hearing. But there were other ways to get out of the country other than with a passport. Geneva knew that running away would make her look guilty, but she didn't care how it looked. She was not going to waste another day of her life in a cell.

It was early evening, and Geneva heard a knock at the door. She zipped up the duffle bag and placed in her closet under her laundry bags. She would take it back to the storage room later. She opened the door and saw Zain.

"I got the food," Zain said.

"Great! I'm starving. They only feed you thick baloney sandwiches in jail," Geneva said.

Zain took the food out of the bags, and they began to eat.

"So, what's the plan going forward?" Zain asked.

"I'm going to talk to Elizabeth. I know her husband is hiding something. They don't have a very good marriage," Geneva said.

"Maybe Elizabeth and Victoria just didn't get along very well, and he didn't want to say anything," Zain said.

"No, there's more to it than Elizabeth and my aunt not getting along. He got nervous when I said that my aunt knew personal information about people. He thought I was talking about more than basic family information," Geneva said.

"When are you going to talk to her?" Zain asked.

"I'm going to visit their home tomorrow morning."

# CHAPTER 40

As she and Su stepped off the bus, Geneva imagined all of the things that could have prevented her from arriving at the bus's final destination. The bus could not have picked them up at the Museum of Science and Industry, it could have had mechanical problems, and broken down, the driver could have gotten lost, but ultimately she knew that the only thing that really would have prevented her from stepping off the bus was herself.

After Zain left and she got ready for bed, Su came by her room and invited her to the casino. Her brain thought about saying no but her mouth said yes. Su made a strong argument that Geneva needed to unwind, and she was correct. But as the dozens of gray haired, limping, cane carrying, casino enthusiasts made their way to the cashier to get chips, Geneva wondered if she really belonged in this place where lost paychecks, lucky charms and sweaty brows were as important, if not more important than the thousands of lights within the casino.

"Let's hit the roulette table first," Su said.

"Doesn't blackjack provide better odds for winning," Geneva said.

"It may provide better odds to win but roulette provides more excitement and more men. And we want both of these in great abundance," Su said smiling.

Su was right, the cheers and sighs of the eight layer deep crowd at the roulette table drowned out the bells and whistles that emanated from the dozens of slot machines that sat just a few feet away. And there were men; some were clean shaven, some had five o'clock shadow, some wore ear rings, some had solid white hair, some sported light reflecting crowns, some wore ties, and some wore jeans. But all of them had two things in common: they had numbers to play and money to lose.

Geneva and Su maneuvered their way to the edge of the table. At eight o'clock, Geneva placed her ten thousand dollars in chips on the table. By ten o'clock, she was stacking up over two hundred fifty-five thousand dollars in chips. As Su continued to scream and to lose her voice, the little ball kept landing on the numbers that Geneva selected.

But the roulette wheel was a fickle bird that changed its flight plan as fast as a streak of lightening could flash in the sky. By midnight, Geneva lost the money she had won only two hours ago. The table attendant was happy to provide her with more chips. Three hours later, the crowd was gone and so was the five hundred thousand dollars in chips that sat in front of her three hours ago.

"You look like you could use some champagne," said a man who wore a pair of pin-striped trousers, a bright red shirt and a black leather jacket.

"No, thank you. I don't drink. I think I need to get out of here," Geneva said.

"You should have some champagne to celebrate," said the man.

"Celebrate what? I just lost a half a million dollars. There's nothing to celebrate."

"You're still standing and at least you had a half a million dollars to lose. That's worth celebrating," the man mused.

"I agree. Let's have some champagne," Su said.

"But we have a bus to catch," Geneva said.

"We have a few minutes. Come on be a sport," Su said.

"After all it's my treat," the man said.

"What's your name?" Geneva asked.

"I'm Paul Jones."

"I'm Su Young Chang and this is my friend Geneva Anderson."

The three choke hands and then headed out of the casino area and into the near by lounge. Paul led Geneva and Su to a booth in the back of the lounge. Paul was not ugly, but he was not a handsome guy either. He wore his hair combed straight back, and it looked like it had too much mousse in it to Geneva. Geneva wished Su had not told him their last names. For some reason, she could not stop thinking that he was just another overweight white guy trying to get lucky with two black women and some free champagne was his ticket to a river of chocolate milk. When the champagne arrived, they made a toast.

"Here's to money. It is alpha and omega," Paul said.

"Yeah, here's to money and more money," Su said.

Geneva said nothing as she lifted her glass and tapped Su's and Paul's.

"Do you come here often, Paul? I've never seen you before," Su said.

"No, not often," he replied as he turned and looked at Geneva. "I've seen you before, haven't I? I've seen you on TV. You were arrested, weren't you?"

"Yes, I was arrested. I rather not talk about it."

"No, problem," Paul said.

"If I make you uncomfortable, you can leave. I'll understand," Geneva said.

"No, I'm not uncomfortable," Paul said.

"What do you do for a living," Geneva asked.

"I manage a hotel," Paul replied. "It must be rough having something like that hanging over your head," Paul continued.

"It's not easy," Geneva said.

"That's why I'm glad that she got out tonight. Getting out can help her to not think about it so much," Su said.

"Distractions provide temporary relief. But I think Geneva would like something more permanent, and I bet she would pay any price to get it. Isn't that right, Geneva?"

"I suppose," Geneva said.

"What would you pay?" Paul asked.

"I'm not sure, why are you asking?"

"You should think about it. You never know when you might have to have an answer," Paul said.

"We really have to get going. Otherwise, we'll miss our bus," Geneva said as she stood up and grabbed Su's arm. After saying their goodbyes to Mr. Jones, Geneva and Su left the lounge and headed directly to the bus stop. They could see people boarding the bus as they approached. While she stood behind Su, she wondered whether she had achieved anything tonight. She did not know for certain. The only thing that she knew for certain was that she had lost half a million dollars and that she shared some cheap champagne with a strange man.

# CHAPTER 41

The next morning, Geneva walked over to the Wilson house to talk to Elizabeth. The bitter cold burned her face and her legs could not carry her fast enough down the street. When she arrived at the Wilson home, she stood on the porch and stomped the snow off her boots. She rang the bell twice. After five minutes, there was no answer. But there were lights on in the house. Geneva rang the bell two more times. Elizabeth Wilson answered the door.

"Hello, Geneva. What are you doing here?"

"I wanted to talk to you for a few minutes about my aunt Victoria," Geneva replied.

Elizabeth stood tightly in the doorway. "What about Victoria?"

Geneva looked directly into Elizabeth's eyes. "I had a few questions that I wanted to ask you. May I come in?"

"Yes, I suppose so," Elizabeth responded.

Elizabeth opened the door wider to let Geneva into the house. Geneva stomped more snow off her feet before she entered. She took off her coat and boots and deposited them on a combination coat and shoe rack in the foyer. She glanced around the foyer and noticed that the hallway wall and the wall leading up the staircase were missing several photographs. The outlines on the walls where the frames once hung were still visible. She didn't notice the empty outlines the last time that she was in the foyer. She wondered whose photographs had been removed from those empty spaces. Geneva turned and faced Elizabeth who stood with her arms crossed.

"Can we sit down?"

Elizabeth turned toward the living room and sat on one of two couches. The living room had oak paneling on the walls and a large oak paneled fireplace. Two mahogany framed couches sat facing each other in front of the fireplace. The room had no pictures or photographs. Geneva sat on the other couch directly opposite Elizabeth.

Elizabeth sat up straight with her legs crossed at the ankles and her arms crossed over her chest. "What do you want to talk about?"

"Do you know of anyone that my aunt did not get along with?"

"I don't think I can help you. My relationship with Victoria was strictly business. She didn't talk to me about any of her relationships with other people," Elizabeth said.

"I spoke with your husband last week. He said that the two of you were visiting your daughter, Monica. Is that correct?"

"You know, Geneva, you need to find yourself a good attorney. And leave the investigating to the experts."

"The experts think I killed my aunt. Someone planted the murder weapon in my room. I'm being framed. I need to find the person responsible for setting me up, and I will do whatever is necessary to find that person. I went to the hospital and spoke with one of the nurses. She said that your husband visits Monica every night, but she could not remember the last time she saw you."

Elizabeth took a deep breath and exhaled. "You have no right to invade our privacy. How dare you. When I visit my daughter is my business and no one else's."

Elizabeth's response confirmed Geneva's suspicion that Bradley lied about their alibi.

"Why was your husband so upset at my aunt's funeral? His face was still red at the repast," Geneva asked, as she stared directly at Elizabeth.

Elizabeth returned her gaze. "I don't know why he was so upset. Some people get upset at funerals."

"Bradley told me that he barely knew my aunt. Why would he get so upset over the death of someone who he barely knew?"

"I'm sure he has his reasons. Geneva, I really have some things that I need to attend to," Elizabeth said, as she stood up and moved towards the entrance of the living room.

Geneva stood. "Elizabeth, you and your husband lied to me and the police about your whereabouts on Monday night. And you're lying about Bradley's behavior at the funeral. And I want to know why."

Elizabeth walked towards Geneva. "Lying? How dare you accuse me of lying; I'm not lying about anything."

"Yes, you are. You and Bradley were not at the hospital. You haven't visited your daughter in a long time. Where were you? Please, tell me the truth. Otherwise, I'll tell Detective Peterson about this."

"The truth. You want to hear the truth. Sometimes knowing the truth is not always the best thing," Elizabeth said, frowning.

"Tell me," Geneva commanded.

"Fine, you're correct I was not at the hospital. In fact, we've not been to the hospital together or done anything else together for the past two years."

"What were you doing that night?" Geneva asked.

"It's not really important what I was doing but rather why I was doing it." Elizabeth walked back into the living room and sat down.

"My husband was in love with Victoria. They had an affair. She ended it two years ago. She never knew that I knew about the two of them."

"Why did she end the affair?" Geneva asked.

"I don't know why. I never asked Bradley. Bradley has not touched me since. He has not hugged me or even held my hand. He wanted her, but he couldn't have her. So he didn't want anyone else."

"I'm sorry about what happened. You must have hated my aunt."

"Yes, I hated your aunt. But I also hated Bradley, and I hate myself," Elizabeth said.

"Where were you the night my aunt was murdered?"

"I didn't kill your aunt. Was I sad about her death? No, I wasn't. But I didn't kill her."

"You still haven't answered my question," Geneva said.

Elizabeth uncrossed her arms and walked over to the telephone that sat on one of the end tables. She made a call with her back facing Geneva.

"It's me. Geneva Anderson is here, and she knows that I didn't visit the hospital. I need to use your name. Are you okay with this?" Elizabeth asked.

Elizabeth sat the receiver down on the end table and turned around. Geneva did not know who was on the other end of the Elizabeth's telephone conversation.

"When a woman's husband is no longer interested in her, she needs to get pleasure from other places. Once a week, I go to a place called, 'The VIL Club'. Have you heard of it?" Elizabeth asked.

"Yes, it's an exotic dance club for women only," Geneva replied.

"The person on the other end of this phone can confirm my presence at the club," Elizabeth said.

Elizabeth walked away from the end table and stood in front of the bay window in her living room with her back facing Geneva. Geneva picked up the phone and placed it to her ear.

"Hello," Geneva said.

"Hello, Ms. Anderson. This is Detective Yvonne Peterson."

Geneva turned towards Elizabeth who still had her back to Geneva. Geneva could not believe her ears.

"Geneva, I was at the, 'VIL Club,' at the same time as Elizabeth. I arrived ten minutes before she did. I got there at nine. We both left at four a.m. I trust that you will be discreet about what I have just told you," Detective Peterson said.

Geneva cleared her throat. "Yes, of course."

Detective Peterson hung up the phone. Geneva listened to the pulsing dial tone for a minute before she hung up the receiver.

"Did you get what you wanted?" Elizabeth asked.

"Yes, I did." Geneva said. Elizabeth turned around and walked to the living room entrance.

"Now, if you don't mind. I have chores to complete."

"Yes, I understand," Geneva said.

She must be a very lonely woman. Geneva wondered why she never confronted her aunt about the affair and why Elizabeth continued to work for her aunt. Everyday must have been agony.

When Geneva left the Wilson home, she decided to talk to Bradley again. She walked passed I-House and continued to Bradley's office.

* * *

Geneva arrived unannounced at Bradley's office. She did not want to give him an opportunity to come up with a convenient meeting or story to weave before her arrival. Bradley agreed to see Geneva. When she entered his office, he was already sitting behind his desk. As she approached his desk, he leaned back in his chair, placed his elbows on the arms of the chair and interlocked his hands across his body.

"What can I do for you today, Ms. Anderson?"

Geneva did not sit down but rather she stood in front of his desk.

"You can tell me the truth," Geneva said.

"Tell you the truth? Wilson said.

"Last week, I visited your house. I over heard you arguing with Elizabeth. I'm asking you to tell me the truth about your relationship with my aunt, and please don't tell me that you barely knew her."

"It's not appropriate to eavesdrop on private conversations, and it's down right illegal to enter someone else's home when you have not been invited to do so," Wilson said.

"I think murder is worse than what I did," Geneva said.

"What exactly did you overhear?"

"I know that your wife has absolutely no respect for you and that you had an affair. What did Victoria know?" Geneva wanted him to admit to having an affair with her aunt, and she wanted to know why it ended.

"Victoria knew that I loved her," Wilson said.

"You had an affair with Victoria," Geneva said.

"I prefer the term relationship as opposed to affair. I cared for your aunt deeply. I was willing to leave my wife. But, Victoria wouldn't let me. She ended our relationship."

"Why?"

"I don't know. I think she was scared. She tried to make me hate her," Wilson said.

"Did you kill her?"

Bradley leaned back in his chair and stared at Geneva for what seemed like an eternity but in reality, was probably only a few seconds.

"Do you think I would tell you?" Wilson said.

"No, I suppose not."

"I believe we are done here," Wilson said, as he opened a file on his desk and started to read it.

"Yes, I suppose we are," Geneva replied.

"Just for the record, I did not murder Victoria. I loved her."

Geneva did not know if she believed Bradley. She did know that she needed to find out why and how her aunt tried to make him hate her. She decided to go back to her aunt's condo to see what she could find.

## CHAPTER 42

Although she hated to ask anyone for help, when she and Zain arrived at her aunt's condo that afternoon, Geneva was glad she was not alone. The pungent odor of the dirty water containing the dead flowers had intensified since their last visit. And this time, Geneva became nauseous within minutes of her arrival. They emptied and rinsed all of the vases in the house before they commenced their search.

Everything in her aunt's condo had a place. The books on the shelves were arranged in alphabetical order, loose paper was non-existent, and even the shelves in the food pantry were labeled. It did not take them long to search through the rooms. Their search did not reveal anything about Victoria and Bradley.

After they searched the condo for two hours, Geneva and Zain returned to Zain's room.

"Maybe Victoria ended her affair with Bradley because of Elizabeth and the Wilson's daughter, and it just doesn't get any more complicated than that," Zain said.

"That's it. That's what was missing from the walls and the living room," Geneva said.

"What do you mean missing from the walls?" Zain asked.

"The Wilsons did not have any pictures of themselves or their daughter displayed. They have several empty spaces on the wall in their foyer and on the wall leading up the stairs. I bet pictures of their daughter used to hang on those walls." Geneva said.

"I think I'm going to have eat my words," Zain said as she looked out of her window.

"What do you mean?" Geneva asked.

"Come here and look at this."

Geneva got up, walked over to the window and stood next to Zain.

"Isn't that Bradley Wilson in your aunt's condo?" Zain asked.

Geneva looked in the direction of her aunt's condo, and she saw a man in her aunt's study looking through the books on the shelves. The man appeared to be Bradley Wilson, but she was not completely sure.

"Where are your binoculars, get them for me quick," Geneva said.

Zain rushed into her closet and searched through some bags and came out a few minutes later with a pair of binoculars and handed them to Geneva. She could clearly see Bradley now. By this time, he had made his way to Victoria's desk. She continued to observe him for another twenty minutes and then he stopped searching the room. He stood in the middle of the study and looked around at everything. Afterwards, he turned off the light and left the room. She looked through the windows of the other rooms, but did not see him enter any of the other rooms on the south side of the condo. She then decided to focus her attention on the sidewalk. Unfortunately, Zain's room only provided a partial view of the sidewalk area in front of the I-House parking lot and not the sidewalk in front of the Nobel House. If Bradley decided to take Fifty-ninth Street back to his house or office instead of Fifty-eighth Street, she would see him walk pass. She was correct. A few minutes later, Bradley walked pass the I-House parking lot and towards Fifty-ninth Street.

"Didn't we just witness a crime? Wasn't he trespassing? Should we tell someone?" Zain asked.

"No, we tell no one. He was looking for something, but I don't think he found it. So I think he may try her office next. I have to beat him to it," Geneva said.

"That's a good idea. We can do that tonight," Zain said.

Although it would be comforting, she did not want to get Zain involved anymore than she had to. *And if Bradley is breaking into places, maybe he's the killer,* Geneva thought.

"I think it would be best if I searched the office alone. After all, it's a crime scene, and I don't think anyone other than the authorities is supposed to be there. There's no point in the both of us getting into trouble," Geneva said.

"Okay, I guess we both don't have to search the office. You can search, and I'll keep a look out from the Main Lounge," Zain said.

Geneva thought about trying to stop her from serving as the look out but decided that it would be a futile effort.

"Okay, then you can be the look out. Let's search her office around eleven tonight. By that time the security guard will either be watching television or sleeping and most people will not be around the office area," Geneva said.

## CHAPTER 43

Bradley placed his daughter's favorite stuffed toy, a baby giraffe, next to her and then tucked the bed sheet and blanket tightly under her bed. He sat in the wing-backed chair beside her bed. It was one of the many items the children's hospital had placed in her room to make it seem less like a hospital room and more like a little girl's room. The walls had a variety of colorful flowers and animals painted on them and dozens of stuffed animals watched over 10 year-old Monica Wilson as she entered her fifth year of being comatose.

Every night for the past five years, Bradley came to tuck her in and to read her a bedtime story. But that night, he did not start reading after tucking in Monica. Instead, he stared as her chest slowly went up and down. She was not hooked up to a respirator. Monica only had a heart monitor, brain wave indicator and an intravenous feeding tube connected to her. As long as she was not brain dead and breathing on her own, Bradley believed that she was simply sleeping and that one day she would wake up. Monica was waiting on something to happen. But he did not know what. When the doctors told him and Elizabeth that she may never come out of her comatose state, Elizabeth stopped visiting her, removed all of the pictures from the house, and cleared out Monica's bedroom. It was as if Monica never existed. Bradley just watched as Elizabeth did these things. He did not know what to do. He let his wife do what she wanted to do and continued to visit Monica everyday.

As the hospital bills accumulated, the doctors suggested moving her to a less expensive facility, but he wanted her to have the best attention possible. Because the university did not pay him the millions of dollars that the other Ivy League universities paid their endowment managers, he had to figure out a way to get the medical bills paid. At first, he felt guilty about stealing money from the university endowment that he had been entrusted to manage and protect, but his guilt faded as Monica continued to celebrate one birthday after the next.

The only thing he could do for his daughter was to keep her comfortable and close to home. Elizabeth never asked where the money came from, and he never volunteered the information. He told one person and that was the woman he loved, Victoria Franklin. But he found out quickly that she did not love him enough to keep his secret. She used the information against him. He continued to love her even after she betrayed him and ended their relationship.

He looked at his watch. It was nine o'clock and the official visiting hours were now over. But the nurses all knew him so they never asked him to leave. He opened the top drawer of the nightstand next to Monica's bed and took out, *The Hobbit*. He leaned back in the chair and began to read to her.

## CHAPTER 44

Margaret returned to her room and found Elizabeth Wilson standing in front of the window with her back to the door.

"What are you doing here?" Margaret asked, as she walked into her room.

Elizabeth did not turn around immediately, so Margaret stood behind her.

"I said what are you doing her?"

Elizabeth turned around with her arms crossed and faced Margaret.

"I want to know what is going on. What are you up to?"

"Someone might ask you that same question since you are the one using the master key and entering resident rooms without their permission," Margaret said.

"Don't play games with me. Did you plant the murder weapon in Geneva's room?" Elizabeth asked.

"I didn't know that they found the murder weapon much less where they found it. How do you know that?" Margaret asked.

"I'm the one asking the questions here, not you," Elizabeth snapped.

"I would recommend that you not worry about my involvement. After all there was no love lost between you and Victoria. You should be glad that Geneva was arrested and not you," Margaret said.

"I have an alibi. What about you? Geneva is not stupid. She is asking questions and investigating Victoria's murder herself. She might find something if she keeps looking," Elizabeth said.

"I wouldn't worry about the questions of a wanna-be-poet. You disappoint me. I thought you had more guts," Margaret said.

"There is a difference between having guts and being suicidal. Things have gone too far. I want it to stop," Elizabeth demanded.

"You're not in a position to demand anything. Now, get out of my room and never come in here again without my permission. When I want to talk to you, I'll contact you."

Margaret walked over to the door and opened it. "Get out, now." Elizabeth slowly walked pass Margaret and left the room.

# CHAPTER 45

Geneva and Zain decided to use the paging and text-messaging features on their cell phones as a way for Zain to notify Geneva when someone approached the office area on the first floor. Zain sat in the Main Lounge facing the main hallway while Geneva made her way to her aunt's office.

After she stood in front of the door for a few minutes, she removed the yellow crime scene tape from across the door and entered the office. She stared at the bare floor. The carpeting had been removed. She closed the door behind her and proceeded to take tiny steps into the room. Even though, the bloodstained carpeting was gone, she remembered the exact position of her aunt's body. She continued to look at the spot as she walked to her aunt's file cabinets.

Geneva searched the file cabinets, the desk, the tables next to the couch, under the furniture and the closet. She looked behind the mirror and pictures on the wall. She even hit the walls to see if they had any hollow spots, and she checked the books on the shelves to see if they contained any hidden items.

She did not know what she was looking for, but there had to be something the police had overlooked. Geneva went through each drawer of her aunt's beloved nineteenth century desk one more time. She noticed that the inside of the bottom drawer was not as deep as the front would make it appear. Also, the bottom drawer had a few scratches around its hook. Geneva lifted the hook and turned it clockwise, but nothing happened. Then she turned the drawer's hook counter clockwise, heard a click and another smaller drawer popped out from the bottom of the drawer.

Inside the hidden drawer, Geneva found a small black book. The contents in the book were written in code. All of the pages except for one had the contents blacked out.

# CHAPTER 46

After she searched her aunt's office, Geneva and Zain went back to Zain's room.

"What did Elizabeth tell you this morning when you talked to her?" Zain asked.

"She confirmed that Bradley and my aunt had an affair. It ended two years ago. Their marriage has not been the same since. He hasn't touched Elizabeth at all since Victoria ended their affair. Elizabeth says that Victoria never knew that she knew about the affair," Geneva said.

"She told you all of this? Why? Doesn't this make her a suspect?"

"It could. She told me because I confronted her about her alibi. She was not with Bradley at the hospital that night. But, she did have someone confirm her whereabouts that night. She hated my aunt, but I also think she hates herself," Geneva said.

"Who confirmed her whereabouts?"

"I'm afraid I can't tell you that but need less to say it is someone who has no reason to lie."

"Did you find anything in Victoria's office?"

"I don't know. I found a black book hidden in a secret drawer in my aunt's desk. The book is encrypted." Geneva handed Zain the book.

Zain flipped through its pages. "This will take some time and a little brain power." She took out a writing pad from her desk. "I think we should get started with solving this code," Zain continued.

Geneva took another pad from Zain's shelf. The book contained a series numbers. The page that did not have it's contents blacked out contained the numbers:

4-18-3-7-8-14-3-5-7-23-6-15-3
7-9-2-8-2-18-3-11-4-18-5-23-6-15-3
3-5-3-16-2-19-4-1-7-13-2
2-18-2-4-5-5-9-23-4-12-7-15-6

Geneva and Zain tried various decryption methods. They matched the numbers up to the numbers on a telephone key pad, the sequential order of the alphabet, added up the numbers and found the average, and saw if all of the numbers were divisible by the same number. After five hours of working on it, Geneva and Zain took a break. Zain rubbed her eyes.

"I think we should call it a night or day since it is now five in the morning. We can try again later today."

Geneva did not respond to Zain. Geneva actually did not even hear Zain. She stared at her written version of the telephone keypad.

"We haven't tried everything yet. Let's try one more thing. We haven't tried to use a combination of the various decryption methods, "Geneva said.

"What do you mean by a combination?"

"We've applied the methods to the numbers individually. We haven't applied two or more decryption methods together." Geneva started out by using the sequential order of the alphabet and then for every other number she applied the telephone keypad. This did not yield any results. Then Geneva reversed the application so that the telephone keypad was first and then the sequential order of the alphabet was applied to every other letter. This approach revealed the names of four people: Greg Underwood; Richard Kirkwood; Deepa Sharma; and Bradley Wilson.

Zain searched the Internet for the names. The Internet search results yielded an obituary for Greg Underwood. The obituary indicated that Greg Underwood died at twelve years old as a result of a hit-and-run accident on November 3, 1994. The newspaper articles indicated that a red car was seen leaving the scene of the accident. No one was ever arrested for the hit-and-run.

The search results also produced an obituary for Richard Kirkwood. The obituary said that Richard Kirkwood, professor and head of the history department at the University of Chicago, committed suicide by hanging himself in this study on May 15, 1985. The obituary said that one daughter and one sister survived him. The newspaper articles indicated that Richard Kirkwood's ten-year-old daughter Margaret Kirkwood found his body. No information came up for Deepa or Wilson except for the fact that he is the in-house manager of the university's endowment fund.

"We know why she might have Bradley's name, why would your aunt have the names of Margaret's deceased father, Deepa, and a deceased little boy encrypted in a hidden book?" Zain asked.

"I don't know, but I'm going to find out." Geneva stood up and walked over to the window. She looked at the Nobel House. "I will start with Margaret tomorrow."

"I can talk to Angela Bannister tomorrow, too," Zain said. "Before she transferred to my department, she used to work in the history department, and she probably knew Prof. Kirkwood. So maybe she can provide some information about his death."

"Okay, but be careful. Don't tell her too much," Geneva said.

"Don't worry. I know what to do. Also, I was thinking that you should talk to Xavier about Deepa. Maybe he can tell us something about her or her and Victoria."

"Absolutely not. I don't want him involved in this. He's not going to talk to me about Deepa. We don't have that kind of a relationship."

Zain smiled. "Are you sure, he won't tell you? You might be surprised by what he's willing to tell you. It all depends on how you ask him. Also, you can use it as an opportunity to talk to him about something other than poetry."

"I'm not going to talk to him about Deepa, my aunt or anything else," Geneva said.

"Okay, then I'll talk to him if you don't feel comfortable."

"No, I don't want him involved. I want you to promise me that you will not talk to him."

"But he might be able to help you. He might know something about Deepa. There's no one else to talk to you about her. It won't hurt to talk to Xavier," Zain said.

"I don't want you talking to him," Geneva said. "I mean it."
"Ok, I won't talk to him. But I think it's a mistake."

## CHAPTER 47

Although Geneva and Margaret had both lived at International House for the past two years, they never really had a conversation that lasted more than five minutes. Margaret was not approachable in either appearance or conversation. Her thin pale frame, piercing blue eyes and long black hair was always a little jarring to Geneva. Geneva had walked passed her countless times and Margaret never made eye contact and never said hello unless spoken to first and sometimes she would not even issue a verbal reply.

Because of their very limited social interaction and Margaret's overall social disposition, Geneva did not have any high expectations for her meeting with Margaret. If Margaret did not refuse her entry, then Geneva would consider the meeting a success.

Next to Margaret's door was a large map of Egypt. Dozens of letter-sized sections were taped together to create the map. The map clearly indicated the location of various Egyptian temples and pyramids. The small bulletin board on her door asked people not to touch the map because it was for her dissertation on Egyptian hieroglyphics. Geneva knocked on the door. A few minutes later Margaret opened the door.

Geneva entered Margaret's room and was not surprised to find that all of the fantasy books, various pictures of wizards, and figurines of mystical creatures were symmetrically arranged to take advantage of every square foot of space within her room. Margaret had that rare talent for making a small space appear to be bigger by simply organizing the items within the given space.

Along the shelf next to her bed, Margaret had pictures of her family. Geneva gazed in the direction of the pictures along Margaret's bed.

"Is that your family?" Geneva asked.

"Yes, it is," Margaret replied. She pointed to the people in one of the pictures. "This is my father, my mother, and my aunt."

"How are they doing?"

"They're all dead," Margaret said.

"I'm sorry to here that. Did you grow up here in Chicago?"

"Should I be talking to you? Weren't arrested for murder," Margaret said.

"The police made a mistake. I didn't kill my aunt."

"Well, obviously someone thinks you did," Margaret said.

"They're wrong! What can you tell me about your relationship with my aunt."

"I really don't think I'm a good person to talk to. I really didn't know your aunt very well. We barely spoke to each other," Margaret said.

"So you never met or heard about her until you came to live in International House?"

"Correct. I never met her until I came here. Who else have you talked to about your aunt?"

"Elizabeth Wilson and some other residents," Geneva replied.

"Well, I really can't help you, and I really have to get back to work," Margaret said.

"Yes, of course. I don't want to take up any more of your time. I was just wondering if maybe your father knew my aunt?"

"Why are you asking about my father?" Margaret asked.

"I think my aunt knew him. Did he ever mention my aunt to you?"

"I don't recall. My father was murdered several years ago."

"I thought your father committed suicide."

"I really don't want to discuss this any further with you." Margaret turned away from Geneva and walked over to her door and opened it. "I really must get back to work."

Geneva stood. "Yes, of course. I didn't mean to disturb you."

Geneva left Margaret's room. She looked at her watch and decided to head downtown for her meeting with Mr. Nicholson. She knew that it would be hard to get any information out of Margaret but it was worth a shot. Because he was her attorney, she hoped that maybe Nicholson could shed some light on her aunt's life

# CHAPTER 48

While she sat in front of Dr. Zimmerman, Margaret adjusted her skirt so the black fabric fell evenly across her lap and down the sides of the chair. She sat straight up with her back pressed firmly against the chair and placed her crossed hands in her lap. This was her Dr. Zimmerman posture that she took great pride in repeating for the past three years. During that time, they played a little game. He tried to get into her head, and she made him believe that he was successful.

They both knew that she did not want to be in his office. But this was one of those silent truths that exist between therapists and their patients. She kept her appointments because her aunt got a judge to believe that there was something wrong with her spending a large portion of her trust fund in a short period of time. The judge decided to extend her aunt's guardianship duties and to require therapy sessions for an indefinite period.

These temporary constraints did not bother Margaret. She still did what she wanted, when she wanted.

Dr. Zimmerman leaned back in his chair with his elbows on the arms of his chair and made a pyramid with his fingertips.

"Last week you mentioned righting a wrong? What did you mean by that?" Zimmerman said.

"I don't remember saying that," Margaret replied.

"Was it related to your father? Last week you said that he was not resting on peace," Zimmerman said.

"I don't want to talk about my father," Margaret said.

"So do you think that he's resting in peace now?"

"I know that he's not. He was murdered and he wants his murderer to pay," Margaret said.

"Margaret, your father committed suicide. He was not murdered," Zimmerman said.

"Murder can be direct or indirect. He was murdered indirectly."

"How do you feel about the death of Victoria Franklin?"

"I feel nothing," Margaret replied.

"What do mean when say you feel nothing? You saw her everyday. You must have some thoughts about her death," Zimmerman said.

"I did not see her everyday. She ran the place where I live but that does not mean that I knew her," Margaret said.

"Your aunt called me. She's concerned about you. She said that the two of you had an argument recently. She is concerned about some of your spending habits lately."

"She's not concerned about me. She's only concerned about when her next spa day or plastic surgery appointment is," Margaret said.

"That's not true and you know it. Your aunt has seen to your care since your father died. She just wants to make sure that you're not letting anyone take advantage of you by buying ancient Ouija boards, magical stones, and tarot cards. You wasted a lot of your inheritance on that kind of stuff. She just doesn't want you to make the same mistake again," Zimmerman said.

"What I do with my money is my business and no one else's." Margaret stood and walked towards the door. "Our time is up."

"Wait, our time is not up," Zimmerman said. "We have thirty minutes left. Let's talk about your dissertation."

Margaret stood still with her back to Dr. Zimmerman for a few seconds and then she opened the door and left the room.

## CHAPTER 49

One of the things that Zain learned when she started attending the University of Chicago was that the staff at the university knew a great deal about the faculty members. But the faculty members knew nothing about the staff. Richard Kirkwood had worked at the University of Chicago for over twenty years before he killed himself.

The offices of the Computer Science department were in Kent Hall in the main university quadrangle. Angela Bannister served as the history department secretary for over twenty-five years and then three years ago she left the history department and came to work for the Computer Science department. Ms. Bannister was a petite African-American woman with light brown skin and the perfect makeup to attenuate her high cheekbones and broad smile. She always wore a two-piece suit to work, and never pants. Zain recognized several of her outfits from the Bloomingdale's and Nordstrom's catalogs.

"Ms. Bannister do you remember Dr. Richard Kirkwood?"

"Yes, I remember him. Why do you want to know? He died before you started at the university," Ms. Bannister said.

"I'm trying to help a friend. Can you help me? What can you tell me about him?" Zain asked.

"The only thing that I can tell you is that Dr. Kirkwood was the head of the history department. Everyone on campus respected him. He was one of the shining young stars in academia at the time. His suicide was a shock to everyone. He was widowed and had one daughter, Margaret. She lives at International House. Do you know her?" Ms. Bannister asked.

"Ya, I know her. I've spoken with her a few times," Zain said.

"She's a strange bird. Does she still dye her hair black?" Ms. Bannister asked.

"Ya, her hair is still black, but I didn't know that it was dyed," Zain said.

"Yes, she's a natural blonde just like her father," Ms. Bannister said.

"You said that Dr. Kirkwood committed suicide. Does anyone know why he killed himself?"

"No one knows why. He appeared to be a very outgoing and happy man. He was always smiling and making jokes. He adored Margaret, and she adored him. I really didn't know much about his personal life. You might want to talk to his former secretary. She worked with him for ten years," Ms. Bannister said.

"Who was is former secretary?"

"Her name is Joanna Quinn. She doesn't work at the university any more. But let me give you her number," Ms. Bannister said, as she flipped through her rolodex and wrote down the phone number and handed it to Zain.

Zain could not believe that, Joanna Quinn, Geneva's half-sister, used to be Richard Kirkwood's secretary.

"Joanna is a very nice woman. When you call her, tell her that you know me, and she'll talk to you. In fact, do you want me to call her for you and pave the way for a meeting?"

"Oh, no, that won't be necessary. I'll call myself," Zain said. "Thank you for the offer and the information. You've been extremely helpful."

"You're welcome. Tell your friend to be careful," Ms. Bannister said.

"I will. I'm going to get out of your hair now. Thanks again," Zain left the computer science offices and headed across the main quadrangle to Swift Hall. Learning that Geneva's half-sister may be involved, helped Zain's decision to talk to Xavier about Deepa. Zain hoped that Xavier's past feelings for Deepa would not stop him from being forthcoming with any information.

# CHAPTER 50

When Xavier Lakemore opened his office door, he greeted Zain with a cheerful hello. Like other non-tenured faculty, Xavier shared an office with three other assistant professors.

Today, his other three office mates were out. However, because there was not enough room between the two rows of desks to fit a chair, Zain had to lean against the front of the desk directly opposite Xavier's desk.

"I hope I'm not bothering you," Zain said.

"No, not at all. I wish we could sit someplace less cramped, but I'm expecting a phone call from London and so I need to stay in my office. Would you like to sit in my chair?"

"No, thank you, I'm fine," Zain said.

"How's Geneva? She hasn't attended workshop, but I also haven't really seen her around I-House since her arrest," Xavier said.

"She's okay under the circumstances," Zain said.

"Do you know why they arrested her?"

"An anonymous caller told the police that the murder weapon was in her room. They searched her room and found a blood stained letter opener. The blood was Victoria's. But I believe that she's being framed."

"So you believe in her innocence?"

"Yes, totally."

"I believe in it too. Is there anything I can do to help her?"

"Yes, I need to know about your relationship with Deepa

Sharma," Zain said.

"Well, I don't know what to say. Why do you want to know about that?" Xavier asked.

"I can't really tell you now. But it would help Geneva if you could."

"There isn't much to tell. We really didn't have a real relationship. She's a hard person to get to know and to care for," Xavier said.

"What do you mean?"

"She is secretive and distant. She keeps people at arms length," Xavier said.

"Did she ever mention Victoria Franklin to you?"

"Deepa never said anything about Victoria. But one day, last September, I saw Deepa walking down the street. I was going to catch up to her but then I noticed she was following another woman in a red suit. So I hung back from Deepa while she watched the woman in the red suit. The woman in the red suit went into the post office and then she went to International House. At this point, Deepa stopped following the woman in the red suit. And she got into her car and drove off. I entered International House. I saw the woman in the red suit standing at the front desk. As I approached the front desk, the woman in the red suit turned around, and it was Victoria Franklin," Xavier said.

"So Deepa was following Victoria."

"Yes, that appears to be the case," Xavier replied.

"Are the two of you investigating Victoria's death?" Xavier asked.

"Yes, we are."

"Well, I hope that the two of you are being careful."

"We are. Don't worry."

# CHAPTER 51

When Geneva arrived at the Nicholson law offices, his secretary, Ms. Michaels informed Geneva that Mr. Nicholson was still in a meeting, but he would be with her in fifteen to twenty minutes. Ms. Michaels was a tall, slender middle-aged African-American woman. Her designer royal blue suit and matching shoes were a testimony to her well-polished image. She wore just enough makeup to highlight her dark chocolate complexion.

Ms. Michaels escorted Geneva into Mr. Nicholson's office. Geneva walked over to the window. Ms. Michaels closed the double doors of the office. Nicholson had the perfect northeast view from his corner office in the Sears Tower. Geneva gazed upon Grant Park, Buckingham Fountain, Navy Pier and the John Hancock building in the north loop and Lake Michigan.

Geneva turned around and surveyed Nicholson's office. The last time she was here she really didn't pay any attention to the opulence of his office. The office contained two overstuffed burgundy leather couches, four dark green winged back chairs, a full bar, floor to ceiling book shelves, and a six foot long mahogany claw footed desk. Geneva wondered if Mr. Nicholson had a family of his own. His office did not have any family photographs. Because she was alone in the office and the door was closed, she wanted to search through Nicholson's desk and pick through the lateral file cabinets.

She began to quiver slightly. Every bone in her body wanted to search his desk. He was her aunt's lawyer. He had to know something. She gave into her impulses and walked over to his desk. Just as she was about to walk behind the desk, the double doors to the office opened and Nicholson walked into the room.

"Ms. Anderson, I apologize for keeping you waiting."

Geneva turned to face him and walked towards one of the brown leather chairs in front of his desk. Geneva's heart was pounding.

"No, problem. I know you're a very busy man," Geneva said.

Nicholson walked swiftly over to his desk and sat. Geneva sat in front of his desk.

"How are you holding up?" Nicholson asked.

"Okay, I suppose. I'm not sure what a murder suspect is supposed to do."

"Stay calm, focused, talk to no one about the case, and listen to your attorney; that is what a murder suspect is supposed to do. Have you been doing these things?"

"Yes," Geneva replied.

"Then you're doing better than okay. Now, let's talk about your sessions with Dr. Zimmerman. He's going to be subpoenaed to turn over your records, but we are going to fight this. But in case we don't win, is there anything in his files that could hurt you? Such as negative comments about your aunt or anyone else?"

"No, nothing like that," Geneva said.

"Good."

"How are you going to prove that I'm innocent?"

"I'm not going to prove that you are innocent. No one can do that. But I am going to cast reasonable doubt about your guilt and that is all the jury needs. The fact that the murder weapon did not have your fingerprints is very helpful. How could someone else know about its location unless they planted it in your room. I have investigators looking into your aunt's life to see if anyone had any reason to want her dead. But so far they have not turned up anything. I'm not surprised."

"Really, I am," Geneva said.

"What do you mean?" Nicholson asked.

Geneva hesitated. "Did you know that my aunt had an affair with a married man named Bradley Wilson?"

"No, I didn't know that. But then again, we weren't close in that way. How do you know this?"

"I spoke with the man's wife. She told me about the affair," Geneva said.

"Ms. Anderson, are you playing detective?"

"I'm trying to find out who murdered my aunt," Geneva said.

"I don't think that's a wise move. Your actions could jeopardize your case. You need to focus on your defense."

"I am focusing on my defense by trying to find my aunt's killer. I just can't sit around and do nothing."

"Yes you can you're not a detective. You should leave the investigating to the professionals. You need to be careful. The person you are trying to find is a murderer. There's nothing that says he or she will stop at one murder."

"Yes, I understand what you're saying," Geneva said.

"I hope so for your sake," Nicholson said.

Because he was not very receptive to her actions thus far, she decided that there was no point in telling him about the black book. For now, only she and Zain needed to know about its existence.

## CHAPTER 52

On Wednesday evening, Geneva sat on her bed with her back against the wall next to the window in her room while Zain sat at the foot of the bed.

"So essentially, Ms. Bannister confirmed the news stories that we read regarding Kirkwood's suicide?" Geneva asked.

"Yes. But she also suggested that I talk to Dr. Kirkwood's former secretary," Zain said.

"Good, who is that and did she provide you with any contact information?"

"Dr. Kirkwood's former secretary was your half-sister Joanna Quinn," Zain said.

Zain handed Geneva the piece of paper that Ms. Bannister had given her with Joanna's home phone on it.

Geneva looked at the paper, and it did indeed contain Joanna's home phone number. When Joanna told her that she did not know Victoria, Geneva found it hard to believe. Her aunt was generous, but she was not generous to the point where she would allow a complete stranger to be the beneficiary on her insurance policy. This proved that Geneva's doubts were justified. But why would Joanna lie about knowing their aunt?

"What else did Ms. Bannister say about Joanna?" Geneva asked.

"Nothing except that she was his secretary for ten years, and that she is very nice. Do you want me to talk to her? Maybe it would be better," Zain said.

"No, I want to talk to her. Anyway, she doesn't know you. At least the two of us have met."

"Okay, you're probably correct. I found out some other information, too. I learned that Deepa followed Victoria one day. So maybe there was something between the two of them. We need to find out more," Zain said.

"How did you find this out?"

"I'd rather not say. It might be perceived as gossiping," Zain said.

"Since when has that stopped you?" Geneva said.

Just as Geneva was about to probe Zain more, someone knocked on her door. She got up and opened the door. It was Xavier.

"May I come in?" Xavier asked.

"Yes," Geneva said as she held the door open and allowed him to walk past her and into her room.

"Zain, I should've known you would be here. I went by your room looking for you. You left one of your gloves in my office," Xavier said. He reached into his coat pocket and pulled out a blue fleece glove and handed it to Zain.

Zain took the glove. "Thank you. I was wondering where I lost it."

"The two of you have seen each other?" Geneva asked.

"Yes, Zain stopped by my office today and we talked"

Geneva crossed her arms and stared at Zain. "I see."

"Well, I think I'll leave the two of you alone to talk," Zain said as she stood up.

Geneva frowned. "There's no need to go. We're not done yet."

Xavier turned and looked at Geneva. "I actually came by to invite you to join me for dinner tonight, my treat."

"I have a lot of work to do. I …" Geneva started to say but Zain interrupted her.

"It can wait. You two should go out. I have to get going. I'll talk to you tomorrow, Geneva," Zain said as she stepped past Geneva and walked to the door.

"Indeed," Geneva said.

"Thanks for bringing my glove, Xavier," Zain said.

"Your welcome."

Zain opened the door and left the room.

"It's six-fifteen and I'm hungry. I didn't have lunch today," Xavier said.

Geneva was annoyed, excited and scared all at the same time. She was annoyed at Zain for going against her wishes and talking to Xavier, excited because he invited her to dinner, and scared because she had absolutely no idea what they would talk about. She prayed that he would not mention her arrest. But she also wondered if he thought she was guilty. She reasoned that he must not since he is willing to be seen in public with her.

"Okay, let me put my boots on and get my coat and then we can go," Geneva said.

* * *

Fifteen minutes later, they arrived at the Italian restaurant. As Xavier reached for the door, Geneva stopped him.

"Wait," Geneva said.

"Wait for what? Do you want to go some place else?" Xavier asked.

"No, not exactly."

"Then what?"

"You're being very kind."

"Are you repaying me by making me starve to death in the cold?"

"No, but I don't want to embarrass you considering my circumstances."

"You could never embarrass me." He opened the door and bowed. "After you," he said.

Xavier sat directly across from Geneva. The silence that accompanied their trek to the restaurant was broken when they placed their orders, but it quickly returned. She knew something must be wrong with her because she really just wanted to sit there and watch how the candlelight on the table made his eyes sparkle.

"I want to apologize for Zain's questioning of you. I didn't ask her to do it," Geneva said.

"If you didn't ask her to talk to me, then there's nothing to apologize for. Zain cares about you. You're very fortunate to have her as a friend," Xavier said. "She told me that the two of you are investigating Victoria's murder?"

"Yes, we are."

"I understand that you want to clear your name, but you also need to be careful. Remember you're looking for a murderer," Xavier said.

"I'm being careful," Geneva said.

"Do you think Deepa had something to do with your aunt's murder?"

"I don't know. I'm not accusing anyone. I just want to find out as much as I can about people who had contact with my aunt."

She wanted to tell him about the black book and her aunt's adultery, but she really did not want to get him too involved.

"I know Deepa can come off as being snobby and arrogant. But she wouldn't harm anyone," Xavier said.

*Even though she dumped him like a hot potato, he's still defending and protecting her. What a waste of his energy*, Geneva thought.

"You're correct. That's her persona, and it does not mean she would hurt someone. But I still need to find out about their relationship, if any," Geneva said. "Do you know anything that might be helpful?"

"Maybe! One night, I was getting some ice out of the ice machine on the loading dock. When I was about to go up the stairs and walk pass Victoria's office, I heard Deepa yelling at Victoria. I stopped and waited. I heard her say she hated Victoria and that Victoria was evil itself. A few seconds later I heard Victoria's door slam," Xavier said.

"When did this occur?" Geneva asked.

"It happened two weeks before Victoria's death," Xavier replied.

"Did you tell anyone else about this?"

"No, people say they hate someone all the time. It doesn't mean they'll commit murder," Xavier said.

"You're correct. It doesn't mean that at all," Geneva said.

Geneva knew that Deepa's hatred for Victoria did not mean she killed Victoria, but she also knew the possibility existed.

"Thanks for telling me about this. I know that it was difficult given your relationship with her and all," Geneva said.

"Deepa and I didn't have a real relationship. She's not the relationship type if you know what I mean," Xavier said.

"So, it was just sex?"

"Yes, basically," Xavier said.

Geneva was disappointed.

"Are you surprised?" Xavier asked.

"It's not really any of my business to be surprised or not. Let's talk about something more pleasant," Geneva said.

"Ok," Xavier said. "Are you still writing?"

"No, not really. I find it difficult to concentrate."

"I'm not surprised. But you should try to write something every day. It will help you to relax."

Geneva and Xavier enjoyed their meal together that night. Xavier told her about his childhood in London and his college years at Oxford. And for a few hours, she forgot about the outside world and allowed herself to get lost in the sparkling eyes of one Xavier Lakemore.

## CHAPTER 53

Geneva returned from dinner to find Zain sitting outside of her door. They went into Geneva's room. Geneva stood with her hands on her waist as she opened her eyes and exhaled all of the air that she just inhaled. She knew that she was not really angry at Zain, but rather she was upset that Xavier was involved.

"Why did you talk to him, when I specifically asked you not to?" Geneva asked.

"I thought he could help, and I was right," Zain replied.

"I need to know I can depend on you to do what I ask, when I ask it. You can't keep going off on your own," Geneva said.

"I'll stop going off on my own, if you stop losing tons of money at the casino," Zain said.

"What…?"

"Don't even try to deny it. Su told me. That's a lot of money to lose in just a few hours. You have a great opportunity to have the life you want. Most of us will not have that chance. You haven't been convicted yet, just arrested. But if you keep doing reckless stuff like Sunday night, then you're just digging your own grave."

"It seems like the money is the problem. If my aunt had not left me that money, then maybe I wouldn't be a suspect," Geneva said.

"The money isn't the problem. It only becomes the problem if you let it. Just like the gambling can become one if you let it," Zain said.

## CHAPTER 54

The next day Geneva arrived at Joanna's apartment.

"I hope I'm not taking you away from something," Geneva said.

"No, not at all. I'm glad you called last night. Let me show you around," Joanna replied.

The apartment had a long rectangular living room. One of the ten-foot walls contained black and white photographs in black frames evenly spaced from the floor to the ceiling. The living room was furnished with a long tapestry-covered couch that was against the wall. The dining room was directly across from the living room. One of the walls in the dining room was also lined with black and white photographs displayed in beech wood frames. The apartment had two bedrooms. Joanna's bedroom featured an oak sleigh bed and matching dresser and chest. Joanna turned the second bedroom into a dark room. The window in the second bedroom had a black covering over it. Like most vintage apartments in Chicago, it had too much heat in the wintertime and no air conditioning in the summer time. Geneva and Joanna left the darkroom and returned to the living room. Geneva took off her sweater before sitting on the couch.

"Would you like some tea?"

"Yes, do you have any iced tea?" Geneva asked.

"Yes, let me fix some," Joanna said.

Joanna went into the kitchen. Geneva looked at the photographs on the wall in the living room. All of the pictures appeared to have been taken at the same location: some sort of a grassy wooded area with a lake and a very large flower garden. The pictures all consisted of flowers, leaves, trees, a lake, sunsets, and sunrises seen from various angles and in different types of light.

As Geneva approached the dining room to look at the photographs in that room, Joanna came out with a tray containing two glasses of iced tea. She sat the tray down on the cocktail table in the living room. Geneva turned, walked over to the couch, and sat. Geneva looked in the direction of the living room wall.

"Those are some very good photographs. Where were they taken?" Geneva asked.

"Those are very old. They were taken at various places," Joanna said.

Geneva sensed that Joanna did not want to talk about the photographs.

"I heard about your arrest. What's happening with your case?"

"I'm being framed. Someone made an anonymous call to the police, and they found the murder weapon in my room at I-House. I'm trying to find out who may have wanted to kill my aunt."

"I understand how you feel, but I also think you should probably leave the detective work to the police. You wouldn't want to make things worse," Joanna said.

"You're probably right, but I need to do something. I just can't sit around and let things happen to me."

"I see. Is there anything I can do to help you?" Joanna asked.

"Yes, I wanted to ask you about Richard Kirkwood. What can you tell me about him?" Geneva asked.

"Richard Kirkwood? Why do you want to know about him?" Joanna asked.

"I found his name among some of Victoria's belongings. I wanted to find out what the connection was between the two of them. I found out you were his secretary. So I thought you could tell me about him."

Joanna drank some of her tea and then sat the glass on the table.

"I don't know what to tell you except that one day he came into the office as usual. Then, he left the office early and went home. The next morning I found out that he had hung himself in his study. No one knows why he did it," Joanna said.

"I read that his daughter, Margaret, found the body," Geneva said.

"Yes, Margaret found his body. She was devastated, and she missed an entire year of school because of what happened. I think the family placed her in a mental hospital for treatment."

"How did her recovery go?" Geneva asked.

"I believe it went well. She finished school, and I think she attends graduate school here at the University of Chicago."

"What about his wife?"

"Margaret's mother died in a car accident when Margaret was two years old. She never knew her mother. Her father was her whole world. That's why his death was so devastating to her. Dr. Kirkwood died over twenty years ago. I don't see how he could have anything to do with Victoria's death."

"I don't either at this point. I just wanted to find out why his name appeared among her belongings," Geneva said.

Geneva did not tell Joanna about the black book. Geneva thought that there was a connection between the two; it was going to take time to figure it out. Geneva took a sip of her tea. She sat the glass on the table. Geneva wanted to find out more about the photographs. She wanted to find out more about her sister.

"Have you always taken black and white photos?" Geneva asked.

"Yes, I like black and white photos. Black and white photographs make the world seem simpler than it really is. Color has a way of distorting reality. Black and white is reality in its purest form."

"Why are there no people in your pictures?" Geneva asked.

"There weren't any around." Joanna stood up. "I received a package yesterday. It contained something that you might find interesting. Let me go get it."

Joanna left the living room and went into her bedroom. Geneva could see her go into the top drawer of her nightstand. Joanna pulled out a yellow envelope and returned to the living room. Joanna handed the envelope to Geneva.

"Take a look at this."

Geneva opened the envelope and pulled out a black and white photograph. The picture showed a light skinned teenage girl with long curly hair in a short-sleeved dress with ruffles at the bottom.

The girl had a big smile and large bright eyes. She was standing on the porch of an old frame house. "Who is this? Is this you? It looks like you."

"That is a picture of our mother when she was fourteen years-old," Joanna said.

"Victoria had the picture. She instructed her lawyer to send it to me upon her death."

Geneva examined the picture. She strained to see a resemblance between herself and her mother. She did not see any. Joanna had a strong resemblance to their mother. Geneva had never seen any photographs of her mother as a young girl.

"Would you like a copy of the picture? I can scan it and print out another one," Joanna said.

"Yes, thank you. I would like a copy of the picture. Is this the only picture you have?" Geneva asked.

"Yes, it is. Do you have any?" Joanna asked.

"No, I don't."

Geneva felt embarrassed to say that she did not have any pictures of her mother. The truth was not only did she not have any pictures of her parents, but she also did not have any of herself as a baby or as a child.

Joanna took the photograph and went into her dark room. After ten minutes or so, she came back and handed Geneva a picture.

"Now you have a picture of her, too. Would you like some more tea?" Joanna asked.

Geneva looked at her watch. "No, thank you. In fact, I really need to be going." She stood. "Thank you for talking with me and for giving me the picture."

Joanna stood. "You're welcome. Feel free to come by anytime. I'm sorry I was not more help."

"Oh, quite the contrary you were very helpful," Geneva said. Joanna escorted Geneva to the door.

Geneva did not want to leave, but she had an appointment with Dr. Zimmerman. She did not tell Joanna that she was in therapy because sometimes people have negative reactions when they find out that someone they know is in therapy. Unfortunately, being in therapy still had a stigma attached to it. A stigma wrapped in doubt and concern. And she did not want Joanna to think something was wrong with her.

# CHAPTER 55

When Geneva got up in the morning, she was tempted to skip her session with Dr. Zimmerman. But after visiting her sister, she decided to go. She needed to talk to someone about Joanna and Xavier.

"Geneva, I want you to know that I'm sorry that you were arrested and that I'm here to support you in any way I can," Zimmerman said.

"Thank you," Geneva said.

"The district attorney wanted to see your medical records. I refused. I have never violated a patient's privacy, and I will not start now."

"Thank you for not releasing my records," Geneva said.

"How did your first meeting with your sister go?" Zimmerman asked.

"I thought it went well. She appears to be a very nice person. We have a few things in common."

"But?" Zimmerman said.

"But what?" Geneva replied.

"I sense a "but" in your response," Zimmerman said.

Dr. Zimmerman always knew when Geneva was not being completely forthcoming. Geneva thought about denying his assertion but changed her mind quickly. Because after all, he was there to listen to the things that she was afraid to tell anyone else or to even admit to herself.

"I feel like there is something she is not telling me. This might be normal considering the fact that we are perfect strangers. But this morning, I was at her apartment. Joanna takes photographs as a hobby. Her walls are lined with black and white photographs. One of the walls in her living room has photographs of what appeared to be the same place. I asked about the photographs, and she said they were old and taken at different locations. Then she quickly moved the conversation away from the photographs. I think she was lying to me, but I don't know why she would or why I have the feeling that she was lying."

"You just met each other. You should not expect too much. The two of you need to get to know each other better. Try not to read into her actions and words so much. You might say something you will regret later," Zimmerman said.

"I know we need to get to know each other, but I'm just anxious," Geneva said.

Geneva's suspicions were also fed by the fact that Kirkwood's name was in Victoria's black book and that Joanna was Kirkwood's secretary.

"Why are you so anxious?" Zimmerman asked.

"I want Joanna and I to get along," Geneva said.

"I think you are getting along, but you have to be patient. Relationships take time. Shared experiences bind people together more than blood. The two of you have not shared any experiences together. An experience can be a lunch or an activity. Your commitment and time will create the relationship that you want. Your worrying will not," Zimmerman said.

"Intellectually I know that you are correct, but the rest of me feels differently."

"What else is going on?" Zimmerman asked.

"I had dinner last night with Xavier. Do you remember me telling you about him?"

"Yes, he is your poetry workshop leader. So you went on a date?"

When Geneva heard him say the word "date", her heart beat a little faster. It never occurred to her that she might have gone out on a date with Xavier. And she didn't know why since that is the thing she had always wanted since she had known him. Maybe the reality was not as good as her fantasy and therefore, her mind could not acknowledge the reality.

"No, I wouldn't call it a date. At least I don't think it was a date. Well, I guess the truth is I don't know if it was a date," Geneva said.

"Did he invite you, did he pay?" Zimmerman asked.

"Yes," Geneva replied.

"Do you know why he asked you to dinner?" Zimmerman asked.

Geneva sat with her mouth partially open. She was embarrassed because she really did not know why he invited her to dinner. She knew why she wanted him to invite her to dinner, but she really did not know his real reasons for issuing the invitation.

"Geneva, are you all right? Did you forget my question?" Zimmerman asked.

"No, I didn't forget it. I just don't have an answer for you."

"That's okay. Tell me how did having dinner with Xavier make you feel?" Zimmerman asked.

As she thought about his question, she smiled. "At first I was nervous, but as the evening went on, I was overcome with joy. I really could have grabbed him and kissed him. But don't worry; I didn't make that big a fool of myself. For some reason, whenever I'm around him, I become caught up in this rapture of euphoria. And when I had dinner with him, I had the same feeling."

"It sounds like you enjoyed yourself and that is a good thing. Will you see him again outside of the workshop?"

"I don't think so. I think I'm also going to stop attending the workshop?" Geneva said.

"Why?"

"I won't see him again because I don't want to start something and then not be able to finish it because of a murder conviction and seeing him in the workshop would only make me feel worse," Geneva replied.

"Don't you see him at I-House?"

"Not really. I rarely run into him and if I am convicted it won't matter."

"May I suggest you put off seeing him again if you feel that is necessary but explain to him why and just take a hiatus from the workshop," Zimmerman said.

"I'll think about it," Geneva said.

# CHAPTER 56

Geneva knocked hard on Deepa's door. Deepa lived in the West wing and her room was adorned with a large map of India above her bed, animal figurines and issues of Vogue, Harper's Bazaar, and Elle on the bookshelves. The shelf directly above her bed held several photographs of herself and people who appeared to be relatives dressed in traditional Indian clothing. One of the photographs showed Deepa standing in a vogue pose next to a red BMW wearing a graduation cap and tassel but no graduate gown. The engraved caption on the frame read, High School graduation 1992.

"What can I do for you?" Deepa asked.

"I wanted to talk to you about Victoria."

Deepa sat on her bed and crossed her legs.

"I'm not sure I can help you. I barely knew her."

"If you barely knew her, why were you arguing with her two weeks before her death?" Geneva demanded.

Geneva pulled out the desk chair, turned it around and sat directly in front of Deepa.

"I don't know what you're talking about. Who told you that we had an argument?" Deepa asked.

"So, you did not have an argument with Victoria?"

"No. I would like to know who is talking about me."

"I would rather not say who told me. When did you last talk to Victoria?"

"During the New Years Day dinner before her death. I'm sure I said hello to her," Deepa said.

"When was the last time that you had a conversation with her that went beyond just hello?"

"I really don't remember. Actually, as I think about it, I never really had any type of a conversation with Victoria except for hellos during the resident social hour," Deepa replied.

Deepa stood and headed toward the door. "I really have other things to do."

Geneva followed her. "I'm sure you do."

Deepa did not open the door but rather she stood next to the door with her hands on her hips. Geneva stepped in front of her and opened the door and left Deepa's room. Because she would take Xavier's word over Deepa's any day, she knew that Deepa lied to her, but she also knew that she had no way of proving it. She decided to try Margaret one more time.

# CHAPTER 57

When Geneva was leaving the West wing, she saw Margaret exit the building. Geneva rushed upstairs and got Zain. She asked Zain to sit in the Main Lounge and let her know when Margaret returned to the building.

Geneva used her aunt's master key to open Margaret's room. She did her best not to disturb the neatly folded clothes in Margaret's drawers. She went through each book on the shelves. She tried not to undo the bed as she lifted it up. Geneva looked at her watch. She had been in the room for thirty minutes and had searched through everything but found nothing of any importance. She knew that there had to be something in Margaret's room. She stood in the room and looked around. Geneva noticed that the picture of Margaret's father was slightly crooked in its frame. She picked up the picture and opened the back. Between the picture and the cardboard matting, there was a letter addressed to Margaret. The letter read:

> Dear Margaret,
>
> I love you, and I'm sorry for the pain that I will cause you. But I just do not know what else to do. I want you to know the truth. I'm doing this in order to protect you.
>
> Your father has made a terrible mistake, and I am being punished for it. Victoria Franklin is blackmailing me. Everyday is torture. I cannot take her threats anymore, and I

cannot afford to keep paying her, either.

I want it all to end. This is the only way. Remember that I will always love you and that I will always be with you.

Love, Dad

Geneva wanted to keep the letter, but she put it back. She did not know what to think. Victoria was a blackmailer and Richard Kirkwood killed himself to escape her. Geneva did not know who her aunt was anymore. Victoria had an affair with a married man, blackmailed a man to the point where he killed himself, and probably made her money by blackmailing other people. Who and what was Victoria Franklin?

Geneva's phone vibrated. It was the signal that she and Zain worked out to indicate Margaret's return. Geneva put the picture back on the shelf and left the room. When she opened the door leading from the hallway to the stairwell, she was face to face with Margaret. Geneva looked into Margaret's eyes and realized that Margaret must have hated her aunt even more than Elizabeth Wilson.

"Excuse me," Geneva said. Margaret stepped aside and let Geneva enter the stairwell. Margaret entered the hallway. As the hallway door closed, the elevator door opened and Zain stepped off the elevator.

"How did it go?" Zain asked.

"Let's go back to my room," Geneva said.

They returned to Geneva's room in silence. It did not bother her that she had just invaded Margaret's privacy. She wished she had taken the letter because she wanted to reread it. Maybe she read the letter wrong. She hoped that she read the letter wrong, but Geneva knew that she had not.

They entered Geneva's room, and she opened the curtains. The snow was falling heavily and the wind rattled the window. Geneva looked out the window and wished that these past few weeks and this night would all vanish just like the snow and wind made the Midway and the buildings outside her window disappear. Zain sat on the bed.

"What did you find in Margaret's room?" Zain asked.

Geneva turned around. Geneva stared at Zain and for a moment and wondered if she should tell her the truth.

"Zain, I don't want you to get involved in something that you may regret later. This situation really doesn't involve you. Victoria Franklin was my aunt and resolving her death and clearing my name are really my burdens. You can still walk away now. So far I have involved you in a burglary. This might become more than you bargained for."

Zain adjusted her glasses. "What are you babbling about? You're my friend. I would do anything for you. Everything I've done, I've executed willingly. Now, tell me what you found."

Geneva sat on the bed beside Zain.

"Victoria Franklin was not the woman I thought she was. She blackmailed people. She drove Margaret's father to commit suicide. Her money probably came from her blackmail schemes. If she blackmailed Richard Kirkwood over twenty years ago, I'm sure she has blackmailed other people since then," Geneva said.

"How do you know all of this?" Zain asked.

"I found a letter behind a photograph of Margaret's father. The letter was written by her father, and it explained why he killed himself."

Zain put her arm around Geneva. "That's unbelievable. I'm sorry."

Geneva began to cry. She could not believe that the woman who helped her so much, whom she admired and aspired to be like was an adulteress and a blackmailer. Victoria used peoples' mistakes in life as a way to make money and in the process caused unimaginable pain. Geneva wondered how many other Richard Kirkwoods there were. How many families did Victoria Franklin hurt? Geneva held on to Zain. She didn't know what else to do or what else to say. The only thing she could think about was the fact that Margaret may have killed Victoria and that her new sister may be involved in Victoria's blackmail schemes.

## CHAPTER 58

On Thursday afternoon, Margaret watched Dr. Zimmerman sit behind his desk. He completed his usual routine. He unscrewed the cap from his pen, placed a pad of yellow legal paper on his desk, and turned on his tape recorder. She often wondered why he just didn't leave these items out from the previous patient's session instead of always taking these things out as if it was for the first time that day.

"Why are you smiling?" Zimmerman asked.

"You make it sound like it is unusual for me to smile. It's a beautiful day. Lots of people are smiling today," Margaret said.

"I suppose it is a beautiful day if you like freezing temperatures, harsh winds and tons of snow. You don't usually smile when you are here. I would even go so far as to say that you're glowing. Is there a reason for this joy?" Zimmerman asked.

Margaret was happy because when she returned to her room last night she felt a piercing sense of disappointment mingled with sadness within her room. Her father's photograph was straight in its frame.

"The truth is out," Margaret said.

"What truth are you talking about?" Zimmerman said.

"You will find out in due time, doctor."

"Margaret, do you think your father would want you to waste your inheritance, time, and intellect on eccentric pursuits?"

"Dr. Zimmerman, do you believe honesty is the best policy?" Margaret asked.

"Yes, it is. Honesty is always the preferred course of action."

"But honesty is always accompanied by pain. Human beings don't like pain as a rule. Therefore, they really don't like honesty. It just sounds good to say that one does," Margaret said.

"Have you experienced some pain recently that resulted from someone being honest with you?"

"No, I haven't but someone else I know has. And this is why I am so happy today," Margaret said.

"Margaret, it's not good to take pleasure in someone else's pain," Zimmerman said.

"But the truth is out and isn't that the most important thing?"

"The truth can be revealed about a certain situation but that does not mean that it is acceptable for you take joy in the pain that results from the truth being revealed."

"That's your opinion and you are entitled to it," Margaret said.

Margaret believed that there was nothing wrong with enjoying someone else's pain if it relieved her own. Margaret never really thought much about other people. People were a means to an end. If an individual did not serve some useful purpose to Margaret, then she never saw any reason to be around that particular individual. Dr. Zimmerman fell into this category. She had to see him because of a court order, not because she wanted to see him. Margaret spent the next forty-five minutes listening to Dr. Zimmerman explain why it is important to care about other people and asking her questions about why she did not. Eventually, her savior arrived, the red light on his desk started to blink. Their session was over.

## CHAPTER 59

Geneva arrived fifteen minutes early for her Friday morning appointment with Mr. Nicholson. He met her in the reception area and escorted her into a conference room.

"The fact that your aunt blackmailed other people does present other suspects. But since you found out that information by entering someone's residence without permission, we can't really use it. Now, if we could find the identity of some of the other people she blackmailed then we will have something to work with. The black book helps us to a point, and we can use that in court. We might even be able to break Margaret on the stand and get her to admit her father was being blackmailed. If we can break her, then we don't have to mention that you found a letter stating such."

"I'm still trying to figure out who the other blackmail victims were," Geneva said.

"Geneva, I am strongly advising you to stop investigating on your own. You may do your case more harm than good. I have investigators. Let me handle it from now on. We don't necessarily have to prove your innocence, we just have to show reasonable doubt," Nicholson said.

Geneva had complete confidence in Mr. Nicholson, but she felt like she was close to finding the truth herself. So she decided to keep investigating. And she always had Plan B.

"What about Deepa and Bradley? They have motives and no alibis," Geneva said.

"There is not much to go on with Deepa. Having an argument with someone doesn't mean anything and although following someone is unusual, she can easily deny it. Bradley is a different story. We might be able to use the fact that Victoria dumped him as a reason for him to kill Victoria, but we need his wife to substantiate the affair. And she might not be willing to do that because of the embarrassment she would endure and the fact that she wants her alibi to remain a secret," Nicholson said.

"So our best hope is finding other blackmail victims and maybe Margaret?" Geneva asked.

"Yes, that's correct," Nicholson said.

# CHAPTER 60

For the next two days, Geneva did not leave International House. She only left her room to eat, shower, and to use the bathroom. She did not visit any common areas. She needed time to think and to plan. And, she did not want to endure the stares and whispers that would greet her if she left her room.

On Monday morning, Geneva dragged herself out of bed and to Dr. Zimmerman's office. She wondered what he would say about Victoria the adulteress and blackmailer. And even though she wondered, she knew that he would never actually express his opinion. He never expressed his opinion about anything. Dr. Zimmerman and Victoria had that one item in common. She has known the both of them for years and has seen them on a regular basis, and she did not really know anything about either one of them.

Dr. Zimmerman looked particularly handsome today. Except for Zain, his color coordination was better than some women Geneva had seen. His beard and mustache were always perfectly groomed. Dr. Zimmerman's tall frame moved like a bird in the sky from his office door to the chair behind his desk.

"I learned some disturbing information about my aunt. And I'm confused about how I should feel," Geneva said.

"What information did you learn?" Zimmerman asked.

"I found out that Victoria had an affair with a married man, and she was a blackmailer who drove another man to commit suicide. In other words, she was not the woman I and the rest of the world thought she was."

Dr. Zimmerman leaned forward in his chair, crossed his hands, and placed his elbows on his desk. The lamp on his desk illuminated his face.

"What do you mean when you say that you are confused about how you should feel?" Zimmerman asked.

Geneva took a deep breath and uncrossed her arms and rubbed her hands on the arms of her chair.

"I want to feel completely disgusted, and I know that I should feel entirely disgusted by Victoria's behavior, but I don't. Part of me admires her tenacity to do what it takes. She broke all of the rules. She made her own rules regardless of who got hurt."

"Why is the ability to break and make rules important to you?" Zimmerman asked.

"Because I've never been able to do it. I've always gone along to get along. Look at how long it has taken me to seriously start writing my poetry."

"I don't think you're confused about your feelings. You know how you feel. You are bothered by your aunt's behavior and at the same time you admire her. There's nothing wrong with that," Zimmerman said.

Dr. Zimmerman uncrossed his hands and leaned back in his chair.

"Are you investigating your aunt's murder?"

"Yes, I am," Geneva said.

"I understand your reasons for wanting to find out the truth. However, I must discourage you from continuing. You might get way over your head. After all you're looking for a murderer, and there's nothing that says he or she cannot kill you."

"I'm being careful," Geneva said.

After spending another forty-five minutes discussing why there is nothing wrong with her having admiration for Victoria. The little red light on his desk started to blink. Geneva's time with Dr. Zimmerman was over. Geneva left Zimmerman's office. She wanted to tell him everything, but it might not be good for him to get too involved.

# CHAPTER 61

Geneva still did not understand why Victoria never told her that she had a half-sister. The only explanation that Geneva could think of was that Victoria did not want her to know about Joanna because Joanna was involved in the blackmailing.

Joanna sat on the couch and Geneva intentionally sat in one of the winged back chairs directly opposite the couch. Geneva did not sleep well last night. Her eyes still felt heavy and she fought the urge to close them.

"I found out some information about Victoria," Geneva said.

Before Joanna could respond, Geneva continued.

"I found out that Victoria was blackmailing Richard Kirkwood and her blackmail led to his suicide."

Joanna stared at Geneva for what seemed like an eternity.

"I don't believe that. It's not true. Who told you that Victoria was blackmailing Dr. Kirkwood?"

"Dr. Kirkwood told me. I read a letter written by him to Margaret. In the letter, he explained why he killed himself. He said that Victoria was blackmailing him and that he could not tolerate it anymore," Geneva said.

Joanna stood and began pacing back and forth in the middle of the living room.

"I don't know why he would write those lies. Victoria would never blackmail someone. She was a caring and generous person. You know that because she helped to put you through school. She has helped other people, too."

"I think we knew what Victoria wanted us to know about her. Why do you doubt Kirkwood, if you did not know Victoria before her death?" Geneva asked.

"How can you believe what he has written?" Joanna asked.

"Victoria had a lot of money. Where did it all come from?"

"I'm not sure that it matters how she got the money," Joanna said.

"It does matter. Maybe someone she blackmailed in the past or in the present wanted her to stop and so they killed her. Why are you rejecting the idea so much? Why are you defending a person that you did not know? You knew Dr. Kirkwood. Why would he lie in his last letter to his daughter?"

"I worked for Dr. Kirkwood and that was it. He was a troubled man. Maybe he imagined that someone was blackmailing him. I don't know. What I do know is that Victoria helped me when I needed it the most, and I don't care about her past," Joanna said.

"She helped you before her death? That means you knew her before she died. You lied to me," Geneva said.

Joanna walked over to the window in the living room and looked out. Her back was to Geneva.

"I had a son. His name was Gregory Underwood, and he was twelve years old. A hit-and-run driver killed him. I suffered a breakdown afterwards. I lost everything. Victoria helped me to recover. She was very generous to me, and she didn't have to be." Joanna turned around with her arms still crossed and stared at Geneva. "So, yes I knew her before she died. But I did not know that she was my aunt. I had no idea that we were related. I lied about knowing her because she asked me to not reveal our prior relationship."

"Why did she ask you to keep it a secret?" Geneva asked.

"I don't know. And I don't really care," Joanna said.

Geneva stood and approached Joanna. "I know that it's difficult for you to listen to what I'm saying."

Joanna walked toward Geneva.

"That's the first accurate thing you've said thus far."

Geneva was startled by the Joanna's statement. "How did she…"

"How did she help me to recover? Is that what you want to know?"

"Yes, how did she…" Geneva could not finish her sentence before

Joanna interrupted her.

"Victoria paid for my medical expenses. She helped me to get admitted into a psychiatric hospital. Victoria helped me to get back on my feet after I was released from the hospital. I suppose you're wondering where the money came from. Well, I don't know, and I don't care and neither should you."

"I disagree. We need to care. Someone murdered Victoria and maybe her past had something to do with it," Geneva said.

"Maybe and maybe not." Joanna walked to the living room entrance. "I want you to leave, now."

Geneva turned and started to walk slowly towards Joanna. Joanna walked into the foyer. Gregory Underwood was one of the encrypted names in the black book. She wondered why did Victoria have the little boy's name encrypted in a hidden book? Was she blackmailing the person who killed the little boy or did she kill him? Geneva thought about saying something but changed her mind. She simply looked at Joanna and continued to walk towards the door. The door slammed behind Geneva causing the stairwell to tremble slightly.

Geneva knew that the conversation would be difficult. She just didn't know how difficult it would be. She felt a great deal of loss as she walked down the snow filled street leading away from Joanna's building.

# CHAPTER 62

When Margaret arrived, the other two were already standing in front of the alter with their arms folded across their chests and their heads bowed down. The secret room beneath Rockefeller Chapel was colder than usual on Monday night. Margaret's limbs started to ache and her hands became stiff as she took five black candles out from the wood box and placed them evenly apart from each other on the altar. She removed the granite bowl and sat it in the middle of the altar in front of the candles. She took out some black hair and placed it on the altar next to the bowl. After she put the wood box back underneath the altar, she lit the candles, removed the top from the granite bowl and placed the black hair inside of it. She removed the *Words of Power* from under the altar, placed it on top of the altar and opened it. She picked up the center candle and used it to set the contents of the bowl on fire. As the flames danced in the bowl, with her arms stretched out, she began to read and the other two individuals repeated after her:

"I call to the mighty Words of Power in the name of Isis
Oh spirit of Isis, hear my call
All most powerful one my thoughts do sing through the universe
Take thine enemy, take her smite
Break her, scorn her in the night
From the night, depths of hell cast your darkness on her
Oh Isis, oh shining star
Touch her, burn her from afar

Revenge now will have its day for thine enemy starts to fray
So it will be!"
After she read the curse, she started to chant:
"Black spirits and white,
Red spirits and grey,
Harken to me I say.
Five points of the Circle, weave the spell,
Red is for break of day,
White is for the noon tide hour,
Grey is for twilight
Black is for the place of power
Great ones, spirits from the past,
Witness it and guard it fast."
She repeated the chant until the fire in the bowl burned out.

After the flame died out in the bowl, Margaret placed the bowl and the book back underneath the alter. She turned around and walked out of the room and into the changing room. The other two followed her.

The three of them removed their robes and dressed in silence. The silence was broken when Margaret said, "Tonight went well. Our objectives are within reach."

"I disagree. My objective, to get that sleaze bucket out of my life, is not happening, and I'm tired of waiting."

"Our patience is paying off. Our objectives will be reached soon."

"Soon, how soon? I haven't seen any progress. Paul is still cheating me and I'm tired of waiting."

"I agree with Heather. I'm tired of waiting too. Deepa is still prancing around while my grandson is under six feet of dirt."

"If something doesn't happen soon, I'm going to take matters into my own hands."

"That wouldn't be a wise move, Heather. You could disrupt the powers that are working on our situation," Margaret said.

"The powers have been powerless so far," Heather said.

"I won't allow you too disrupt all of my hard work," Margaret said.

"You won't allow me. I don't take orders from people like you. I give them."

"Ladies, fighting amongst ourselves isn't going to help us any. It will only make matters worse."

"You're wrong Angela. It's not arguing that's going to hurt us. It's people thinking they understand things that are beyond their abilities," Margaret said.

"By people, I suppose..." Before she could finish, Angela interrupted Heather.

"You know it's late, and we should all get going. I think some rest will allow cooler heads to prevail," Angela said.

Angela picked up Heather's coat and handed it to her. "Let's go," Angela said.

Heather put on her coat and walked up the stairs with Angela behind her.

## CHAPTER 63

Geneva tried to follow Xavier's advice but could not do so entirely. She spent some time on Tuesday writing, but she also spent time thinking about what her next steps would be to clear her name. Darkness had already arrived outside as she printed out the final version of the poem that she started early in the morning. Just when the poem finished printing, someone knocked on her door. She opened the door and found Joanna standing in the hallway.

"Hello, Geneva. Is this a bad time?"

"No, it's not. Do you want to go downstairs? We would be more comfortable," Geneva replied.

"Actually, can we talk in your room? I won't take up much of your time," Joanna said.

"Sure, but just so you know, my room is messy and small," Geneva said.

Joanna pulled the chair from under the desk. Geneva sat on her bed at a distance from Joanna.

"I want to begin by apologizing. Victoria helped me so much after the death of my son. Greg was my whole world. When I lost him, I lost my world," Joanna said. "You know the pictures on the wall in my living room? Those are pictures of the grounds at the hospital were I stayed. I keep them to remind me not to go back."

Geneva moved to the other end of the bed and sat directly in front of Joanna. "I know how you feel about Victoria. There's no need to apologize. She helped me, too."

"I do have to apologize. I told you several lies. I think I know why Dr. Kirkwood committed suicide. One day I left a book that I was reading at the office. I came back later that same evening. I caught Dr. Kirkwood and a male graduate student half naked and kissing in his office. Later on, Dr. Kirkwood begged me not to tell anyone. I told him that I would not. He was a good man. He was a fair man. Back then, homosexuality was not accepted, and even if it was, he still would have gotten into trouble because he was involved with one of his students," Joanna said. She stopped and shifted her eyes downward. "I didn't keep his secret. I told Victoria about the incident. About six months later, she purchased her condo at the Nobel House and a new car. I never really thought much about it. I don't know if she was blackmailing him or not. I honestly don't know."

"But it's a big coincidence," Geneva said.

"Yes, it is," Joanna replied.

# CHAPTER 64

After spending the past two weeks practicing with Xavier and waiting for over ten years to get retribution against the woman who locked her in a locker for eight hours, ruined her prom by spilling red punch on her white dress, and endlessly gloating about her victories, Zain thought that tonight she would be the victorious one, the one basking in the glory of winning but she left disappointed. Heather did not show up to fight her that night. Zain wondered if this was some sort of a new game Heather was playing. Maybe Heather knew she was looking forward to fighting her and did not show up in order to deny her the opportunity. How cunning was Heather.

Xavier came with Zain to The Mouliner. He did not know why Heather did not show. They both knew that it was not like her to back away from a fight especially one she expected to win. Xavier drove down Lake Shore Drive towards Hyde Park. But instead of exiting at the Museum, he exited at Forty-seventh Street.

"Where are we going?"

"I think we should run by Regents Park and see if Heather is at home and find out why she didn't show up," Xavier said.

On the way into the building, Xavier ran into one of his students who let him and Zain into the building. Xavier did not bother to call upstairs to Heather's or to even check the directory for her apartment number. He led the way directly to her apartment. Obviously, he had been there before.

Xavier knocked on the door but there was no answer. After knocking six times, he turned the doorknob. The door was not locked. He opened the door.

"Should we do this? Isn't this breaking and entering?"

"Yes, but I don't think Heather will call the police. We can wait for her to get back."

Xavier entered the apartment and the two of them quickly realized that they would not have to wait for Heather. She was home. She was sitting in a chair, her head bent back and her mouth and eyes wide open while blood dripped from her wrists and pooled around the chair. She was dead. Zain thought she would have been happy that she would no longer have to see or think about Heather. Instead, disappointment ran through her veins like water flows down a river during a high current. Zain was disappointed because Heather choose suicide instead of fighting whatever it was that was bothering her.

# CHAPTER 65

Geneva went to Zain's room early Wednesday morning with her laptop in hand. When she arrived, she set up her workspace on the bed.

"So, do you really believe that Joanna had nothing to do with Victoria's blackmailing schemes?" Zain asked.

"I want to believe her, but the only way that I can know for certain is to follow the money and see if any of it leads to her."

"What do you have in mind?" Zain asked.

"I want to check my aunt's accounts to see if we can figure out where the money came from and if any money went to anyone else, including Joanna. My aunt left me her online access IDs for her accounts. We can start with those. But first I want to start with her incoming and outgoing phone calls. Can you access the university phone system to check her office phone?"

Geneva knew that Zain could easily get into the university phone system because she worked for the Information Technology office on campus, and she always took great pride in being able to access all of the university servers. Geneva just wasn't sure she would access them on her behalf.

"Yes, I can do that. What am I looking for?"

"For now, just look for calls either to or from Deepa, Bradley, Elizabeth, and Margaret and any calls received or made at a high volume. I will do the same for Victoria's cell and home phones," Geneva said.

"Should we include Joanna on that list?" Zain asked.

"Yes, include Joanna, too," Geneva said.

Geneva accessed the website for Victoria's cell phone provider. Because she did not know the password, she decided to try the reset password feature on the website to see if she could access Victoria's online account. Like most online password reset systems, it only asked for the last four digits of Victoria's social security number and a security question. The security question in this instance was Victoria's place of birth. Geneva entered the requested information, and she was allowed to perform an onscreen password reset instead of a password reset via the account holder's email. After she reset the password, Geneva was able to access Victoria's cell phone history.

The online reporting tool displayed the detail for calls received, made and missed. Geneva sorted the calls received by caller last name and date. The sort revealed that during the past thirty days before her death Victoria received exactly one hundred and three calls from three different phone numbers belonging to Bradley Wilson. These calls were all labeled as voicemail messages. Geneva performed the same last name and date sort for the calls made data, and it revealed that Victoria made a variety of calls to herself and I-House, but she only made one call to Bradley. The missed calls data reported that Victoria had missed twelve calls from Bradley. There were no calls received, made or missed from Deepa, Elizabeth, Margaret or even Joanna.

To see the call history for Victoria's home phone, Geneva went to the website for Victoria's landline telephone provider. However, Victoria had not previously created an online account and so Geneva could not utilize the password-reset feature. Instead, she created a new online account for Victoria's home phone.

The online report showed that Victoria received exactly twenty-four calls from Bradley and that Victoria only made two calls to Bradley during the thirty days before her death.

"What do the office phone records show, Zain?" Geneva asked.

"They show that Victoria received twenty-three calls from Bradley and eight from Deepa and that Victoria made one to Bradley and one to Deepa during the thirty days before her death. Also, I checked Bradley's office phone records, and they show that he made eighteen calls to Deepa during the past month," Zain said.

"Victoria's cell and home phone records show that she received over one hundred calls from Bradley before her death," Geneva said.

"So, we've confirmed that Bradley was still trying to make contact with Victoria and that he obviously knows Deepa. The question is why he was trying to contact them," Zain said.

"Maybe the account history will help us to answer that question."

Zain pulled her chair next to Geneva so she could see the laptop screen. Geneva accessed the checking account first. The account's transaction history showed monthly cash withdrawals of five thousand dollars and wire transfers in the amount of one hundred thousand dollars from Victoria's Swiss bank account. The Swiss bank account's transaction history showed monthly incoming wire transfers from two separate accounts in the amount of fifty thousand dollars each. Geneva clicked on the individual transaction listings to see the payment information for the wire transfers. The payment information showed that Bradley and Deepa sent the wires. Zain recorded the two funding account numbers.

"I think we should examine the wire transaction history for these two accounts," Zain suggested.

"How are we going to do that?" Geneva said.

"I can search the Federal Reserve Data Archive Database. The database is stored on the servers of a private data warehousing center," Zain said.

"Should I ask how it is that you can access the servers of a data warehousing center?" Geneva asked.

"No, you shouldn't ask," Zain said smiling.

Geneva knew that Zain used be involved in a hacking club. The club members used race each other to see how fast they could hack into a computer. She said that they never did anything malicious; rather, they just broke through the firewalls of various systems for the thrill of it all. Geneva assumed that the data-warehousing center was probably just one of the many challenges that Zain successfully met.

The Fed wire system is an electronic funds transfer service. It links twelve Federal Reserve banks to approximately ten thousand depository institutions nationwide. Banks send wire transfers on behalf of individuals and companies. Whenever an individual or a company initiates a wire transfer, it goes to the Federal Reserve Bank. Fed wires can be domestic or international transactions. Fed wires do not physically transfer money; they only transfer ownership of the money. The Federal Reserve serves as the middleman and provides security for the banking institutions on both sides of the transaction. The Federal Reserve archives all of its Fed wire transaction history. Because its servers can only hold so much data, the Federal Reserve contracts with a private data warehouse center to store its data.

Zain went over to her laptop and accessed the data-warehousing center contracted by the Federal Reserve to store its archived history. Starting with Bradley's account number, Zain searched the Fed wire archive database by account number. The search results showed that on a monthly basis Bradley's account received incoming fed wires in the amount of one hundred thousand dollars, too. And with the exception of the last withdrawal, which was for eight thousand dollars, his account also showed weekly cash withdrawals for five thousand dollars.

Zain reviewed the wire instructions for the one hundred thousand dollar transaction, and the payment instructions revealed that the money came from an account in the Cayman Islands belonging to an entity named Heal the Children Foundation.

Zain wrote down the account number belonging to the foundation and then performed another account number search. The search results showed that the Heal the Children Foundation account received monthly fed wires from the University of Chicago Endowment Fund.

The data for Deep's account showed that she transferred fifty thousand dollars from her checking account to Victoria's Swiss bank account and that she made weekly cash deposits in the amount of five thousand dollars and that the last cash deposit was for eight thousand dollars. The deposits were made only one or two day after Bradley's cash withdrawals for the same amounts.

"It looks like we got some answers from this labyrinth of accounts," Zain said.

"Sort of! We know that Bradley and Deepa were paying Victoria and that Bradley is stealing money from the endowment and that he might be paying Deepa. We have the links, but the chain is not complete. We need to confirm that Victoria was blackmailing Bradley over his embezzlement from the endowment and why is he paying Deepa? Is she blackmailing him or is he paying her for something else?" Geneva said.

"I think Bradley is either paying Deepa for sex or to keep quiet about his affair with Victoria," Zain said.

"But Elizabeth knows about Bradley's affair, and is he working alone to take money from the endowment or does he have a partner?" Geneva said.

"But, Bradley doesn't know that Elizabeth knows, and I think he's working alone. He's the manager for the fund, and he has full discretion regarding the investments and probably the charity donations, too," Zain said.

"That's true. But we still have a lot of maybes and only a few absolutes. We need to get more information, and we need to get it from the source," Geneva said.

"What are you talking about?" Zain said.

"What time is it?" Geneva asked.

"It's one-fifteen," Zain said.

"Good! Radio Shack is still open. Let's go. We have some shopping to do," Geneva said.

## CHAPTER 66

Friday night, Margaret sat in her rusty Volkswagen Beetle on the Midway across the street from Rockefeller Chapel. From her position, she had a clear view of the chapel. Two hours ago a note was slipped under her door that was composed using letters cut out of magazines and legal size paper. The note read:

To preserve your secret, come to the basement of Rockefeller Chapel tonight at nine o'clock.

Margaret had no intention of being in the basement at nine o'clock, but she wanted to see who else would show up. Margaret looked at her watch. The time was nine-fifty.

A few minutes later, a navy blue Toyota Camry pulled up and parked in front of Rockefeller Chapel. Margaret took out her binoculars to see who was in the car. The car sat with its headlights on. After five minutes had passed, Bradley Wilson stepped out of the car. He slowly walked up to the double doors of the chapel. He paused for a moment and then he used both of his hands and opened both of the heavy wooded doors at the same time. Margaret wished she could be a fly on the wall in that basement, but she would have to settle for just knowing that the sands had begun to flow through the hourglass and soon the end was near. She turned the key in the ignition and enjoyed the sound of her tires crushing the snow beneath them.

\* \* \*

The double glass doors leading to the reception hall were wide open and the room was dark. The only light penetrating the reception hall came from the small hallway in the basement. Geneva stood far enough away from the doors and the light from the hallway so she would not be seen. So far her plan was not going well. Margaret was a no show. It was nine fifty-eight, and there was no sign of Bradley.

Seconds later, she heard footsteps coming down the stone staircase that led into the basement. Bradley appeared in the doorway of the reception hall.

"Stop right there," a voice said. She used an electronic voice changer to disguise her voice. It was one of the little gadgets that she and Zain picked up at Radio Shack.

Bradley stopped after only taking three steps into the room. "Who are you?"

"Who I am is not important. What I know is," the voice said.

"What exactly is it that you think you know?" Bradley asked.

"I know that you will continue the same financial arrangement that you had with Victoria with me," the voice said.

"Why would I do that?" Bradley said.

"Because you don't want the university's board of directors to find out about the Heal the Children Foundation account in the Cayman Islands," the voice said.

There was silence after she made her statement. She wanted to break the silence, but she knew that would reveal her eagerness. Her silence means she controls the situation. She must not give away her control.

"Can we make a deal? What if I give you a one time payment, and we call it a done deal?" Bradley asked.

"No, I want a hundred thousand a month, just like Victoria," the voice said.

"What? I only paid Victoria fifty thousand dollars a month," Bradley said.

"I am not Victoria. She is dead," the voice said.

"But she understood my situation. I have a daughter and the money is for her medical care," Bradley said.

*He's trying to make a deal. He's desperate*, Geneva thought. If he had murdered Victoria, he wouldn't be trying to make a deal.

"I don't care about your personal problems. Why are you paying Deepa Sharma?" the voice asked.

"That's not relevant," Bradley snapped.

"It is relevant if I asked the question. Why are you paying her?" the voice asked.

"I have a difficult relationship with my wife," Bradley said.

"So you are paying her for sex?" the voice said.

"Not exactly. Her cooperation. I'm paying her for her cooperation," Bradley said.

Bradley was correct that it was not relevant. But, Geneva wanted to know. She might need to use the information later.

"What about a one time payment of two million dollars?" Bradley asked.

"Won't someone at the endowment notice a large amount of money like that missing?" the voice said.

"The university's endowment is the third largest in the country, and I approve investments worth hundreds of millions of dollars every day. Two million dollars is a drop in the bucket. No one will notice," Bradley said.

Geneva decided that Bradley could not help her anymore. It was time for him to leave.

"It's time for you to go," the voice said.

"Do we have a deal?" Bradley asked.

"You need to go, now!" the voice demanded.

Bradley hesitated for a moment, but then he turned around and left the reception hall. Geneva heard him walk up the stairs.

## CHAPTER 67

After Zain adjusted the volume on the recorder, she stood up, and an arm grabbed her from behind and a needle pierced her left shoulder. The pain in her shoulder was brief but the acute weakness that started in her feet and rose to her thighs was constant. The room became dark, and she fell to the floor. The coldness of the floor chilled her right cheek. The noise from the recording equipment being smashed on the floor reminded her that she was not alone. The footsteps walked away from her and the door closed. She was alone, unable to move and in the dark.

\* \* \*

At ten-thirty, Geneva heard someone walk down the stone staircase. It was too early for Deepa to be arriving. But seconds later, Deepa appeared in the doorway.

Using the voice changer, Geneva said, "You're early."

Deepa did not respond. She started to walk into the reception hall. "Stop. That's far enough," the voice said.

Deepa stopped. But then she turned around, walked forward a few steps and closed the doors. Geneva heard the lock on the door snap into place. Deepa turned on the lights. Geneva squinted and raised her hand to her eyes when the bright lights came on.

"So it's you. Did you really think you would get away with this?" How stupid do you think I am?" Deepa asked.

Geneva removed the voice changer from her neck.

"I don't think you're stupid at all," Geneva said.

"How did you find out about me?" Deepa asked.

"Victoria had your name in a black book that she kept hidden in her office," Geneva replied.

"You're lying. I searched that office top to bottom. If there was a black book there, I would have found it."

"There was a book. It was hidden in a secret drawer in her desk," Geneva said.

"Give me that book," Deepa demanded.

"How long did Victoria blackmail you?"

"Too long, now give me that book?"

"First, tell me how you killed her?"

"Why? So your little friend can record it? I took care of her, but nice try."

"You must have hated my aunt. She was using your money to pay for her condo, her car, her designer clothes, and her vacations. That must have made you sick."

"You don't know the meaning of hate."

"What was she holding over you?"

"When I was in college, I accidentally hit a twelve-year-old boy with my car, and he died. I left the scene. I confided in your aunt. She advised me to keep quiet about the accident. So I listened to her. One month later, she started demanding money. After eleven years of payments and living in fear, my trust fund is just about gone. I had to stop her. Your aunt was ruthless. She used anybody to get what she wanted even her own relatives. I will not allow anyone to control me any more including somebody like you. Now, give me that book," Deepa demanded.

"Was the little boy's name, Greg Underwood?"

"Yes, it was."

"Why did you kill Devon Bannister?"

"I didn't kill him. He had an asthma attack."

"But you let him die. You used the neuromuscular agent on him and then left him to die."

"People die for worthy causes all the time."

"You used the drug because you wanted her to know that she was being killed. You wanted her to suffer."

"Suffering wasn't good enough for her," Deepa said smiling.

"If she blackmailed you for eleven years, why did you wait so long to kill her?" Geneva asked.

"I didn't kill her. I wanted her to suffer."

"Why did you frame me? I didn't do anything to you."

"Like you said, I paid for everything including your education. She raved about you, and anything that she cared about, I didn't."

"You enjoyed it didn't you?"

"You're right. I did. I wanted her to have the same experience that I've had for the past eleven years. I wanted her to know what it's like to not be able to do anything and to be in constant fear while someone else held your life in their hands," Deepa said.

A shiver of fear ran through Geneva. Her muscles tensed up, and she stood perfectly still.

"You're not going to get away with this," Geneva said.

Deepa walked towards Geneva.

"You're wrong. I am getting away with this," Deepa said, as she pulled a syringe out of her pocket with her right hand and lunged it toward Geneva's chest.

## CHAPTER 68

As Deepa's arm came toward her, Geneva grabbed it and the two began to struggle. Geneva pushed her on to one of the rectangular tables in the room. The syringe fell out of Deepa's hand. She threw her weight against Geneva and pushed the both of them to the floor. Geneva kicked her and managed to get loose from her grip. As Geneva began to stand, Deepa grabbed her ankle and pulled her down again. When Geneva hit the floor, Deepa quickly turned around and positioned herself on top of Geneva and started to strangle her. Geneva was unable to break Deepa's grip.

Seconds later, glass flew into the room. Detective Peterson used a fire extinguisher to break the stain glass doors. She ran into the room and hit Deepa on the back of the head with the extinguisher. Deepa collapsed on top of Geneva. Peterson dropped the extinguisher and pulled Deepa off Geneva. Geneva coughed and staggered unsuccessfully to her feet until Peterson took hold of her left arm and helped her up.

"Are you all right?" Detective Peterson asked.

"Yes, I think so. What are you doing here?"

"I followed Bradley Wilson. I thought he killed your aunt. I hid behind a wall next to the bathroom. I heard the two of you fighting."

"She denied killing my aunt but she tried to kill me. I don't know if she did it or not."

"When we question her, we'll find out."

"I need to see if Zain is alright," Geneva said.

"You go. I'll stay here and watch her," Peterson said.

Geneva turned and walked away from Peterson. Before she reached the doorway, she heard a scream. Geneva turned around and saw a short, chubby, white man with slicked back hair standing over Peterson holding a baseball bat. The man poked Peterson with his bat.

"I guess we don't have to worry about her for a while," the man said.

Geneva started to back away from the man. He pointed his bat at her.

"Don't move," he commanded.

"Who are you?" Geneva asked.

"Don't you remember me? We met at the casino. I know all about you. And I knew your aunt. In fact, I knew her so well that I killed her."

"You killed her? Why?"

"I wanted her to make me a full partner."

"You helped her to blackmail people?"

"I was her whole operation. She didn't want to get her precious hands dirty. I'm the one who followed and photographed professors who liked to have affairs with their students. I'm the one who told her if any faculty or staff members showed up at the hotel with people other than their spouses."

"She wouldn't make you a full partner so you killed her?" Geneva said as she stepped towards him.

"Yes. She wanted to stop and shut down the operation. She was just going to toss me aside. No one tosses Paul Jones a side. No one. Especially people like Victoria and Heather Whitmore. People who don't like to get their own hands dirty."

"You killed Heather Whitmore too? Why?"

"I was her partner in The Mouliner. She wanted to get rid of me too. So I got rid of her first."

"You framed me and not Deepa?" Geneva asked.

"No, that was the divine Ms. Sharma. You see she injected Victoria with some drug and then she left. I went in and did the rest. The good doctor here just wanted Victoria to be temporarily, blind and paralyzed. I wanted her to be permanently dead. I left the letter opener. I guess the good doctor came back and took it and then she had the bright idea to frame you," Jones said.

Geneva looked in the direction of where the syringe was lying on the floor and dashed to retrieve it. Jones threw himself towards her. She grabbed the syringe and turned on to her back and jammed it into his chest as he fell towards her. His mouth opened wide and his eyes became big as he fell forward and hit the floor.

Geneva did not know what was in the syringe. She hoped that he was not dead. She walked over to Jones, bent over and picked up his wrist to feel his pulse. Geneva let out a long sigh. He was not dead.

She went over to see if Peterson was all right. Peterson was alive and moving slightly. Geneva went through Peterson's pockets and found her cell phone and called the police. Afterwards, she ran to see about Zain.

## CHAPTER 69

Two weeks later, the snow had melted, the temperature was in the forties and the sun shined brightly over Chicago. Geneva took her time walking to Dr. Zimmerman's office that Monday morning. Paul Jones, the hotel clerk at the Ramada Inn was charged with the murder of Victoria Franklin and Heather Whitmore. Deepa Sharma was charged with one count of first-degree murder, breaking and entering and tampering with evidence. Because there is no statute of limitations on murder, the murder change was for the hit-and-run death of Gregory Underwood, Joanna's son. Geneva had found her aunt's murderer and her nephew's murderer. She felt a great sense of relief and sadness. Geneva looked up at the street sign and realized that she had just passed Dr. Zimmerman's house. She turned around and walked back two blocks.

Bradley was arrested for embezzlement from the university endowment. He was being held without bail. He fully exonerated Elizabeth. Last week Monica Wilson died. After the funeral, Elizabeth resigned from I-House, and sold her home.

When Geneva entered the waiting area, Dr. Zimmerman opened his office door. Geneva thought she might get to see another patient exiting, but he was alone. She entered his office. They sat down and her session began. Geneva told Dr. Zimmerman about how she and Zain caught Deepa and Jones.

"Geneva, I'm glad that you solved your aunt's murder, but I must admit that I think your actions were very reckless. You endangered your life and the life of your friend," Zimmerman said.

"I understand what you're saying, but it had to be done. If I had not decided to take matters into my own hands, then I would be facing prison and two murderers would still be at large. I have no regrets," Geneva said.

"Do you hate Jones for killing your aunt?"

"No, I don't hate him. My aunt caused her own death. A person cannot expect to get away with hurting and threatening people without facing the consequences one day. I feel sorry for Deepa because she really has lost everything now. I understand her hatred for my aunt. My aunt literally controlled her life. Deepa wanted to take that control back," Geneva said.

"Have you started writing again?" Zimmerman asked.

"Yes, I finished eight poems so far."

"That's wonderful."

"What do you have planned for the rest of the day?"

"I'm having lunch with Xavier."

"Are you looking forward to your lunch?" Zimmerman asked smiling.

"Yes, very much," Geneva said.

"Good, I'm glad to hear that. You deserve it."

## CHAPTER 70

The Oakwoods Cemetery at Seventy-first and Cottage Grove was scattered with small patches of snow barely hanging on while the sun beamed them away. Oakwoods Cemetery contained the graves of several famous African Americans including Chicago's first African American mayor, Harold Washington. The cemetery used to be one of a handful that allowed African Americans to be buried in it. Richard Kirkwood asked to be buried at Oakwoods because it was the closet cemetery to the University of Chicago.

Margaret brushed off the small patches of snow from around her father's headstone. After cleaning off the stone bench next to the grave site, she took out an oversized cushion from its plastic bag and placed it on the stone bench. She sat down, crossed her legs at her ankles and placed her hands in her lap.

"Dad, it's finished. The two people who hurt you have been punished. You can rest in peace now." She closed her eyes and began to chant.

"As the fire is hot
Imperium (absolute power)
As the fire burns the candle
Imperium
As the candle burns away
Imperium"

# About the Author

Bernadette Steele is a native of Chicago, Illinois. In 2004, Bernadette moved into the International House at the University of Chicago. The multicultural environment and gothic architecture of I-House and the U of C campus inspired her to write her first murder mystery novel, *The Poetry of Murder*. This novel is the first in a continuing series of mystery novels featuring the protagonist, Geneva Anderson.

Due to a difficult childhood, Bernadette did not finish the sixth grade and never attended high school. She earned her Bachelor of Arts degree in English from the University of Illinois at Chicago in 1993 and her Master of Science degree in Technical Communication and Information Design from the Illinois Institute of Technology (IIT) in 2003. Currently, she is pursuing a PhD in Technical Communication at IIT and has an expected graduation date of 2010. She plans to pursue a career in academia.

Printed in the United States
126749LV00002B/23/A